THE SENSE OF OTHER

A LOVE BEYOND REASON NOVEL

ANGELINA KALAHARI

FLAME PROJECTS

978-1-7390851-0-0
Flame Projects
London
www.flameprojects.com
The Sense of Other

"A PROFESSOR AT UNIVERSITY told me there were no original stories in the world. But I feel with *The Sense of Other* Angelina Kalahari has created something original I've not read before." – Clare Kissane

For Liam

Thank you for reading *The Sense of Other*.

I trust you enjoy reading the novel as much as I've enjoyed writing it.

To receive occasional email notifications about freebies, new stories and novels, YouTube videos, podcasts, short stories and much more, you can subscribe to my Newsletter here - https://angelinakalahari.com/contact/.

You can also email me at angelina@angelinakalahari.com or please go to the end of this novel for more details.

The first thing you'll receive upon subscribing is an exclusive novella called *Diary of Naomi, a Desert Elephant* - it's the story of what happens to ellie Naomi.

*Elephants in Namibia are the toughest in Africa.
But orphaned elephants are the toughest still. And
they need to be.*

*All elephants must travel great distances to find
food to live on and they're renowned for their mag-
nificent memories and deep emotions.*

We first come across ellie Naomi in *Under a Namibian Sky*. In the novella, *Diary of Naomi, a Desert Elephant*, we discover what happens when she finds the people responsible for making her an orphan.

PROLOGUE

SOMETHING IS WRONG. I know it straight away. I know
it with the knowingness when you just know something,
and you don't know how you know it. The knowing lives
inside me, without pictures, without words.

But there are sounds. Mother's sounds. Her voice. And other voices - deeper, scary. Mother is scared. Her heart is beating
fast, thrumming in my ears, her breathing faster.

Suddenly, an enormous squeeze clutches me. It's too tight.
More follow. The grip feels suffocating and angry, unlike the
warm, fuzzy rubs and hugs from Mother when she's overcome
with love for me. The squeezes are much stronger. They feel
serious and not loving at all, getting even tighter now and more
frequent.

I want them to stop, but they don't. Why don't they stop?

It's hurting now, and one follows the next more and more
rapidly.

Mother's sounds are loud.

Has something happened to us? Something terrible?

The squeezes are even tighter. Mother isn't stopping them. I want to stop them, but I don't know how.

I'm moving now, moving away from the warm weightlessness that is my home, down a very narrow place. It's slippery, and I can't stop moving no matter how hard I try. My shoulders are squashed up towards my head.

Many other unfamiliar voices join Mother's - scared or excited. I can't tell which.

My body moves even further down the narrow place. Somehow, I don't know how, I'm sure I'll see Mother's face soon. I'm happy about it, looking forward to it. But as soon as I relax, rough hands grab my head and yank me quickly through the narrow place. My body gulps air. My legs and arms flail without my permission.

A bright light hits my eyes. I can't focus on anything, but I know the skin I feel beneath me belongs to Mother. Her sounds are nearer, clearer and happy. She's making cooing sounds. Her soft hands touch me all over, touching my toes and my fingers as though she's checking that all of me is here, that I'm safe.

I'm still struggling to breathe in this place, but just as I'm enjoying Mother's hands on my body, her skin beneath me and the bright lights around me, other, rougher hands take me away from her.

I feel instantly cold.

Peculiar, pungent smells are all around me. I can hear a strange sound and realise it's coming from me. I'm crying, yes, but it's shocking. The actual sound of my voice makes me cry even louder. I don't remember ever hearing it, and I've cried many times before.

I wonder if others can hear me, too? If Mother can hear me? Will she come to me?

Mother doesn't come. But another someone - like her - with unfamiliar smells and sounds - comes. She picks me up. She makes soothing sounds and gently sways me from side to side. It's comforting, and I stop crying. I look up at her and see she's smiling.

In her eyes, the thing that's wrong with me recognises me in the reflection and smiles back. It's much bigger than me, and I'm glad it's here. I feel safe now.

It likes the nurse. Its grin becomes broader.

I focus on it and hardly hear her whispered words, but understand she's misinterpreted my smile.

"You're a lovely little boy, aren't you? And so bright, I see, already smiling, and you just born. But poor little thing, your ma's just a babby herself. I wonder what'll become of you?"

CHAPTER 1

I'M PRETTY SURE I'M dead. There's a slim chance I'm wrong. But I think I'm a goner from all I've read and seen.

I get up from where my body is lying on the tiles in my bathroom. A dark-brown string attaches my navel to my body.

Wait. What?

I look down at myself. I'm definitely attached to the body on the floor that belonged to me mere moments ago. Weirdly, I feel no sorrow for that body. It's gross lying there, rolls spilling over the tracksuit bottoms. I try to grab the brown string, but it's fuzzy, and I can't get hold of it. How to get rid of it? I'm distracted by how amazing I feel. My attention isn't on the string for very long. I can't seem to get a hold of myself.

For the first time in my life, I feel light. It's not my weight, which has become even more unmanageable over the last months since the incident. This feels more like a lightness in my being, and it's fantastic. I'm so free. There's no heaviness or tightness in my chest. I'd stopped noticing the anxiety through the years. But it's been with me, part of me like another limb, since birth.

Hadn't I known that something dense and dark lived within me from the moment I was born? Something much bigger than me that had somehow bound me in invisible chains. I could never break through them, and the darkness repelled people, including my mother. Nothing I did could fix it, and then the other, the thing I tried with my whole being to hide, to control, would surface and create havoc in my life.

But from the beginning, the darkness invaded every part of me - my mind, my body, my being. I felt imprisoned even when I wasn't in jail as an adult - stifled, and some days, I was drowning in it.

No one understood it. No one could help. The doctors diagnosed something, and I took the tablets, though I knew they wouldn't help. Not really. They only controlled the voices for a while.

My voice was the only thing about me that could fly free. But though I seldom used it, I couldn't help noticing the surprise on people's faces when they heard me, as though they couldn't believe something so beautiful could come out of someone like me. I couldn't blame them, and I never did.

The manic giggle building up inside me rushes out. It reminds me of the cackling from the weirdos I'd tried to avoid in prison. But I can't stop myself. I'm bent over, laughing and laughing. I'm laughing so hard I don't notice the change around me at first.

A scream of fright and delight escapes me when I straighten.

Everything has changed. I'm in my bathroom, but it's not as I know it. A bright light is inside the room, so bright I want to shade my eyes. Like a rip in the fabric of reality, it layers over the world I had known before, obscuring it, and I have to squint to see through it. In the far distance, I see figures, but I know at once they aren't alive in the world I'd just left. I may have known these people, and I wonder if my mother is among them.

I'm still trying to make out the individuals when I feel *him* more than I see him. He's standing beside me, facing the figures as though he, too, can see them, and I know he can.

I'm shocked he's here because he's the last person I thought I'd ever see again, not least when I die. But he stands beside me so still, so unlike the man I'd experienced when he was alive.

All at once, I remember that night. How he'd clowned around, hiding behind corners to jump out and pretend-scare me as we walked down the dark street to my flat. I liked his playfulness, but it confused me too. He was like no one else I'd ever met.

Even though he was with that woman, I could tell he was gay. What was her name? Oh yes, Isabelle. How odd that I'd remember her name now. But it's such a lovely name. Feels like I'm singing when I say it. Such a gorgeous couple. Pity they weren't a proper couple. But then, if they were, he wouldn't have joined me.

I thought he'd be like all the other guys in costumes, prison or the others in the clubs. They wanted me for just one thing. I loved them for the attention and moments of love I wanted to believe they felt for me. Isn't love what we all crave? I'd seen a TV programme once about love being the one thing all beings on this planet want. But I hated those guys too because I was never anything to them in the end - just a piece of meat to satisfy their sexual perversions. They made me feel even worse afterwards, as though I was nothing and didn't matter. It took me weeks to recover from each meeting, but it was always worth that tiny moment of love, if only in my brief fantasy. I couldn't be too hard on those guys who used me. I used them too.

But *he'd* surprised me. He genuinely wanted a friend. A straight friend, he'd said. How he'd known I wasn't gay, I'll never know. I guess it's one reason I was such a hit with queers - they like the fantasy of turning a straight man, don't they?

But he was different. I believed him. His otherness and sincerity shone out from him like a torch. We shared stories and the drugs. He had loads with him in his rucksack, and when we got to my flat, I offered him some of mine to return the favour. But mostly, I preferred my cider and cigarettes. Thankfully, he had money and bought more at the corner shop before we reached my place, so I had plenty for the night.

How could I have known he'd fucking die in my bathroom? And he broke my fucking toilet seat.

But it was an accident, wasn't it? I'd convinced myself and others that it was. It's the one thing my voice is excellent for. Its beauty can mesmerise people.

I wait for the surge of anger I always feel at the memories of that night, but there's nothing. I feel nothing but freedom and joy and something else I can't name, something overwhelming. But I don't dwell on it too long because I'm aware of him standing beside me, so still as though he's waiting for something.

When I look at him, he turns and smiles at me.

I remember that smile. So beautiful, warm and pure. He seems happy to see me. His blue eyes sparkle just as I remember.

His voice is musical and I'm surprised to hear it kept the soft Scottish accent when everything else about him seems different, radiant, awesome.

"How are you, Lee?"

At first, I'm not sure I heard him because I didn't see his lips moving, but his voice is in my head. Or is it one of my voices? Did I imagine it?

But he asks again, and I know it's different here, wherever we are. Though they look like the bodies we'd had when we were alive, our bodies work differently here.

I answer him in my thoughts.

"I don't know. I feel different. Where are we?"

He smiles at me again and continues to look at me with that expression I can't read.

"You know you can't return to your body, right?"

I look down at the brown string, but it's gone. So, this really is it. I'm definitely dead. It's not a dream, as I'd secretly hoped.

I think I'm nodding. I hope I am.

"Yes, I figured. But where are we? Why are you here?"

He closes his eyes for a moment.

"I think you know. We're waiting now. It won't be long. Be patient, okay?"

I'm too caught up in the lightness I feel to pay him much attention. I enjoy this unfamiliar sensation and want to stay inside it in case it disappears soon. So, I say nothing, but I'm aware he continues to look at me. His stillness is disconcerting, but whatever...

I don't want to remember that night anymore, and he reminds me of it. Under normal circumstances, I would be angry now. But I'm not mad. There's only this lightness inside me and something else, the other sensation I can't name. It's enormous, though, but not scary and nothing like the darkness that had lived inside me my whole life.

I feel so alive and also somewhat sleepy at the same time. I close my eyes for moments, and as I do so, I sense, rather than see, many light forms like him surrounding me. We're moving now, faster and faster, so fast I think I'm nothing more than a beam of light.

When I open my eyes again, we're somewhere else, somewhere I feel I should know, and the knowing gnaws at the back of my mind. I'm aware others surround us, but me and him stand alone in a white chamber. All around the walls are massive panels, like TV screens.

I turn around and around, staring at the screens.

Lights dance in them, flicker, and then a scene appears...

CHAPTER 2

MOTHER IS ON THE phone. She's walking back and forth in our small living room. Her hair is standing up even more than usual, and she runs a distracted hand through it now and then. Mother seems so alive. She's by turns, talking quickly and then being very silent as she listens to the other person speaking.

Something is wrong. It has something to do with Uncle.

I sit between Conor and Mary on the red sofa, watching the telly. Mother said we could watch cartoons. Conor and Mary are watching cartoons. But I prefer to watch Mother.

Something terrible has happened to Uncle. He's died.

Mother's conversation on the phone goes on for longer than I've ever seen. She cries and yells and then becomes quiet, watching us as she listens to the other person talking. She's moving her eyes as if she is thinking about what to do with us. I can still hear Uncle's voice from last night asking her what she's going to do with the older two.

Conor and Mary don't look at her. They're watching the telly.

When the phone call finally ends, Mother sits on her chair at the table, resting her head in her hands. Her shoulders shake, and I think she's crying, but she's quiet.

The front door buzzer goes, and Conor gets up to answer it, his eyes fixed on the telly until the very last moment.

Mother doesn't move, nor does she look up when Grandmother walks into the room. Grandmother is bigger than Mother, but they look very similar. Grandmother's hair is shorter. It's a little curly, just like Uncle's.

She seems angry and unhappy.

"Look at the state of the place, Moreen. Don't you ever clean up?"

Conor returns to the sofa beside me, his eyes glued to the programme on the telly again.

Mother lifts her head. She looks like she has a cold.

Grandmother's hands are on her hips.

"Why are you so upset? He wasn't your son. He was mine. I should cry like you. But I can't, can I? No, because I have to come here to sort you out. He tried, you know. He tried to help you, but you're such an ungrateful little cow, aren't you? And now he's gone, my beautiful son. I'll never understand why he came here last night. What happened here? Did you fight with him, as usual? Why couldn't you just love your brother?"

I don't like the sound of Grandmother's rough voice. The immense darkness in me awakens again and stirs, but it doesn't come out this time. It doesn't even peep at Grandmother as it did at Uncle last night.

Mother says nothing.

Her eyes are moving over us again, as she did earlier. She's become like Conor - quiet, distant, drawn into herself.

Grandmother sighs and sits down on Conor's chair at the table.

"Right, let's get the kids clean first. Do you have hot water in this godforsaken place?"

Mother gets up. She moves slowly as she leaves the room. Moments later, the sound of running water comes from the bathroom.

Mother comes to stand in the doorway.

Her voice sounds strange and soft, like she's lost a great battle.

"Conor, time for your bath."

He keeps his eyes stay on the telly as he follows Mother from the room.

Grandmother comes to sit in the space Conor has left on the sofa. She picks me up and gingerly holds me on her knees, staring at my face, unsmiling. Her eyes are sharp, like Uncle's, but as she's squinting at me, I only now see how shiny they are through her lashes.

Suddenly, she turns me this way and that, really looking at me as though she's seen something interesting in me. I can't imagine what. She's still not smiling, so it's not something funny. Then, abruptly, she turns me around, so I'm sitting on her knees, facing the telly again.

Conor comes back. He takes Mary's place as she slides from the sofa to follow Mother to the bathroom. Conor smells of clean soap. His face glistens, and his dark-blond wet hair has been combed neatly back, the longer bits tucked behind his ears. It looks smarter than his normal hair, which stands up in all directions because he never combs it. He's wearing clean clothes. A white T-shirt under a red hoodie, and jeans with

proper socks and trainers. The clothes look new. I wonder where he got them from. He watches the telly again, fully absorbed as though he'd never left. I can feel Grandmother staring at
him, but he doesn't respond to her inspection of him.

When Mary comes back into the room, she's clean, too. Her dark hair, still wet, hangs in two long plaits beside her head. Her face is gleaming, and her lovely green eyes are sparkling. She's dressed in pink tights under a pink dress, a grey woollen cardigan over the top, and white trainers, like Conor's. She smiles and comes to sit beside Grandmother.

I can't stop staring at her. She looks like an angel.

Mother walks over and takes me from Grandmother's outstretched arms. Grandmother is offering me as though I'm something foul.

We walk to the bathroom. I already know I won't enjoy having a bath. I didn't like it at the hospital, and I'm pretty sure nothing has changed since then.

As always, I'm astonished to hear my voice. As always, it's piercing and loud and hurts my ears, so I cry even louder.

Mother offers no sympathy. Unceremoniously, she strips and dumps me into the bath. Thankfully, the water only just covers my legs, and it's lovely against my skin. I stop crying as Mother scoops the warm water over my body while holding my head upright with her other hand. I love the feeling of the soap suds on my body. But when she tries to wash my hair, my loud voice erupts again and startles me into a crying fit.

Mother ignores my loud screaming and finishes washing my hair. She lifts me out of the bath and wraps me in a big towel. I like the feeling of her attention on me, of her arms around me. I stop crying. She's holding me close and making soft cooing sounds, gently running her hand over my back. It's a wonderful feeling, even with the towel between her hand and my body.

Her wet tears on my neck add to the warmth.

"God help me, help us, my darling Lee."

Mother's voice is soft and sad, for my ears only.

"It'll all stop now. He can't hurt me anymore. There'll never be more like you. No more babies from him. I did love him. I really did, but I'm grateful he's gone. Is that so wrong of me?"

CHAPTER 3

THE BIG CALENDAR HANGING on the back of the living room door has a red circle around fifteen May. Apparently, that's my birthday.

There are three days left until I'm three. It sounds old. But Mary must be about my age because I can now walk and talk like her, and I'm proud of it. I still wear a nappy, though.

Mary has been making a fuss for ages, dropping hints about my birthday surprise, teasing me. Mother's said nothing, and Conor, who is now going to school, hasn't mentioned it either.

The place is empty without Conor, and Mary and I always look forward to his arrival from school each day.

But he doesn't really play with us anymore. If anything, he's become even more withdrawn than he was before. He does his homework at the table as soon as he comes in. Then, he changes out of his school clothes, hangs them neatly on a hanger on Mother's wardrobe door, and makes himself cheese toasties before sitting in front of the telly 'till bedtime. Still, his presence at home is nice.

Mother's been having one of her turns for days now. Most of the time, she just sits on the sofa, staring out the window. It's different from the turns she has when there are many empty bottles on the floor. This time, there are no bottles.

Mary and I climbed up on the chair we pulled over to the window. We wanted to see what Mother was staring at. But it's just the row of trees in the street. The trees are pretty - green with flowers. Maybe Mother enjoys looking at them, Mary suggested. I think Mary's right.

Mary's making cheese toasties on the grill. I helped her pull the chair down the hallway into the kitchen so she could reach it. I know she was planning on stacking them on the plate and taking some to Mother, but we're too hungry. We eat them as soon as they're cool enough to touch. Mary says we need to leave some for Conor when he comes home from school, so she doesn't use all the bread and cheese. Mary says Grandmother will come later. That means more bread and cheese, nappies for me, and other things we need.

Grandmother comes on the same day every week. That's how Mary knows when she'll be here. And although it's good because she brings food and stuff with her, it's also bad because she comes later, when she knows Conor will be home too, so she can make us all have a bath.

I still don't like it, but I don't cry anymore. Everyone says I'm too big for crying now, so I don't. Grandmother also yells and screams at Mother, which doesn't help with her turns. They always seem much worse after Grandmother's been.

The front door buzzer sounds three short buzzes, then silence, then three short rings. Conor's code. Mary skips down the hallway to open the big front door to all the flats for him. I follow behind and wait in our doorway. Conor says nothing as he pushes past us, but he gives each a pat on the head. We follow him back to the living room, where Mother is still sitting like a statue since yesterday. I don't think she even slept last night. She didn't come to bed.

Conor walks over and bends towards her, but she pays him no attention, stares out the window. He puts his hand on her shoulder, but she doesn't move. He sighs, takes his bag with schoolbooks over to the table, and starts his homework.

Mary and I sit down on the floor in front of the telly. Earlier, Mary brought her blanket from her mattress to sit on and wrap around us. It's still quite cold, and the floor is even colder. Mary has the remote, and she's skipping through the channels. She finds CBBC. At least there's something we can watch, a cartoon. Mary loves cartoons.

I watch Conor. He's unmistakably still a child, but his skinny body already carries the energy of a man.

The door buzzer goes again. Conor gets up to answer it and follows Grandmother back into the living room, helping to carry the bags of groceries.

Grandmother squints at Mother and asks no one in particular, but we all know she's talking to Conor.

"Has she been like it all this time?"

Conor nods and goes back to his homework.

Grandmother puts down the bags and walks over to Mother. She bends down and stares into Mother's eyes. Grandmother's stare can be pretty intimidating. But Mother doesn't move or flinch, even. Grandmother stays like that for moments.

She steps back, her hands on her hips, still contemplating Mother.

"Conor, take the kids to the bathroom and get them ready for bath time."

Conor gets up, takes Mary's hand in one of his and mine in the other. He pulls us up and walks us to the bathroom.

My stomach feels funny. I wish I didn't have to have a bath. But I know Grandmother will come to bathe us soon, as usual.

Conor puts the plug in the hole and fills the bath with warm water. The steam makes my breathing feel weird.

Mary undresses quickly and gets into the bath, but I can't get my T-shirt over my head. It's stuck, somehow. With Conor's help, I wriggle and finally free myself of it and my nappy.

As Conor helps me into the bath, we hear a thunderous smacking sound. All three of us stop and turn towards the door. The smack came from the living room.

We listen to Grandmother's voice speaking low and fast.

"Snap out of it, will you? You have three kids to look after. Who knows why you kept them all? And all by different fathers. Dear God, Moreen, what were you thinking? Now you've dragged me into your mess, haven't you? What's wrong with you? You're not like him. You'll never be like him, so stop pretending. I can't do this anymore. This is your choice, your responsibility."

The low talking is punctuated with more loud smacks. I can't work out if Grandmother is clapping her hands together or if she's actually slapping Mother.

I look at Conor. His face is white and drawn, and he doesn't look at us. He's washing Mary, instead. Her eyes are enormous and dark, and she stares at the door. She appears unaware that Conor is lifting each of her arms as he washes them.

He hands her the pink cloth.

"Here, wash your privates," he tells her and turns his attention to me.

Mary soaps the pink cloth, gets up and turns her back to us as she washes between her legs. Conor washes my hair, face, and body, then hands me the cloth and soap he used with the same command he gave Mary.

But we all stop dead when we hear Mother's scream. I've never heard that sound before. It's a long, drawn-out wailing scream that seems to get louder and louder.

Conor closes the toilet lid and sits down on it, his legs drawn to his chest, his arms tight around his knees, his head buried between them. Mary sits down in the water. Her body mimics Conor's exactly. I'm on my knees in the bath, holding onto the side with both hands.

Mother's scream goes on and on. How does she not need to breathe?

Even though I try not to, I cry. I can hear Mary crying too, but Conor is quiet, and so is Grandmother. I can't hear Mary's voice anymore because Mother's voice is hurting my ears. My crying gets louder, and now my sound hurts my ears even more. Mary is sobbing when Grandmother suddenly appears in the doorway. Her face is red, her eyes are glittery, and her hair is wild, standing in all directions.

Grandmother's voice is terrifying in our small bathroom. "Shut up!"

Mary and I stop crying, but Mother is still wailing and wailing in the living room. It sounds as though she'll never stop.

What did Grandmother do to her? She might do it to us.

My lower lip quivers again, but I swallow the tears. Mary starts to sob again. The movement of her body is making small waves in the rapidly cooling water. Either that, or she's shivering as uncontrollably as I am.

Grandmother's voice is still too loud for the small room.

"Conor. Pull yourself together. Get the kids to bed. Now!"

Grandmother leaves as quickly as she's appeared.

Mother's howling sound has entered my head. I can't get rid of it. It takes over my entire body. I start to shake, and Conor grabs my arms just as I slip into the bath. He lifts me out of the tub and holds me tight against him. But my body seems in spasm, and I can't stop shaking. My legs and arms are rigid.

Conor takes me to the bedroom and lies me down on my mattress opposite Mother's bed. He's holding my head up, his other hand on my chest. It feels hot where his hands are touching me. He's making shushing sounds and occasionally glancing at the door. I don't think I'm making any sounds, but I must be if he's shushing me.

Mary appears in the doorway. Her eyes are enormous in her small, porcelain face, but she isn't crying anymore. Her wet hair clings to her head and neck, and she shivers in the threadbare towel around her tiny body. Conor motions with his head for her to come in. He puts a quick finger to his lips, a warning to stay quiet.

The immense darkness in me takes over.

The me that is me is gone...

CHAPTER 4

THE SCENES FADE, AND the panels are impossibly white again, innocent even, as though they had not just been alive with awful snippets from my life. Watching it like this magnifies the horror of it, as though it happened to someone else. It shocked me.

I stare at the screens. I'd shudder if I could.

The neglect, poverty, and wrongness of that life were appalling. I didn't fully understand how dreadful it was when I was in it, and I was too young to see it.

I thought I'd be sad, but I am not. There's a flicker of sorrow, but I seem unable to access emotions in the way I did when I was alive. I'm not indifferent to the suffering I saw on the screen of my life, but I don't feel the urge to rant about it as I once did. In place of the grief and anger, I now feel only a calm acceptance and an overwhelming wish to help. It might be too late for my family. But there are others. If I could ease their pain, their suffering, it would... what?

What would it do? For them, for me, especially now? I'm no longer part of their world, am I?

But even as I ponder this question and feel my brain will explode, I can't deny the wrongness, the injustice, the horrendousness. No one should suffer like that. I don't know the answer.

Something else occurred to me earlier when I was watching my family. I've often heard of free will - we all have free will. If it were true, why would anyone choose that life? It's one of the many questions that's appeared in my mind. It amazed me because I don't think such profound things. Perhaps it's because I'm no longer constricted in my body that my mind is unchained too?

I'm surprised to find myself sitting on the floor, my head in my hands.

So, I'm not as unaffected as I thought.

He is still here, extending a hand. He's helping me up. His eyes look deep into mine, and I can read his compassion clearly.

His voice echoes slightly through the chamber, but I realise it's only in my head.

"Are you alright?"

I can't answer because I don't know if I am alright. I can't get a grip on what's happening to me. Should I be scared? But I feel nothing other than the lightness I find so distracting. Something else distracts even more, so everything else recedes. But I can't name it or recognise it other than feeling that it's massive. It's like a warm blanket that envelops me, and I suspect it's always been there, always kept me safe even when things got dangerous.

How did I not know about it?

All I have to compare it to is the colossal darkness that had lived inside me all my life, because I sense how much more enormous this new thing is. The darkness somehow kept me safe, but I knew it was conditional. I had to submit to it, obey it, allow it to come through me. I knew it did terrible things to people, but I couldn't stop it.

Why me? I'd often wondered why it chose me to enter the world, and I do so again. Guess I'll never know.

But the enormity of what I'm feeling now is very different. There's nothing dark in it. It feels... I don't have the words to describe it, but perhaps "pure" comes closest to what I'm experiencing.

I notice *him* again. He's remained here, his hand on my shoulder, as though he's waiting for something.

Oh, right? I remember he asked something.

I look up at him. He's still taller than me, even here.

He repeats his question as though he senses my inner struggle.

I direct my thoughts to him.

"I think I'm okay. Things are so different now, and I'm confused because I don't know what's happening."

His beautiful smile is back.

"Nothing to worry about. You won't be harmed, and you're not in trouble."

How often have I heard the phrase, "You're not in trouble." It usually meant I was way past being in trouble, so it brings me no comfort from him.

He must sense my unease because he takes a step closer to me.

"I mean it. You won't be harmed here. We're all here to help."

"Help with what?"

His eyes rest on me, and I see knowledge swirling inside them, but he says nothing.

I wish I had the words to ask the many questions sitting at the edge of my mind.

And the darkness... I'd named it the Glome.

It took me over entirely for the first time in the scene I just saw. It's when I knew I'd lost myself, that I'd never be who I thought I could be - normal. I'd given up then. There was no point in fighting it. I'd known from that moment my life didn't belong to me.

But to see it play out like that... it was worse than I'd imagined.

The sense of having it inside my body, of being unable to counter it, descends on me. But it's fleeting, and as I look down at myself, I appreciate anew I no longer have a physical body. As though my thoughts can direct my feelings, the sensation evaporates like smoke.

I stare at the panels, praying the power I had known so well can't penetrate the room. But there's no sign the Glome entered through the panels or that it's near me here. I don't want it to show itself, don't want it to infect me again.

I didn't think I could feel emotions here since the lightness in my being has been so distracting, and also the other sensation, the one I can't name yet.

But now I realise I'm ashamed of the Glome, of the darkness. I have always been ashamed of it, as though it was my dirty secret. I can't believe I'm still trying to hide it, even though it's no longer a part of me.

An unwelcome thought occurs.

Perhaps it's only left temporarily and will return when I least expect it. Isn't it what happened when I was in my physical body?

The tablets sometimes kept it at bay, or more likely, the Glome pretended they did.

For the first time since my death, I'm suddenly terrified. Haven't I known the darkness, its enormity, and how nothing is immune to its power? It's an overwhelming force. Why would it disappear just because I'm dead? Since my birth, it's been with me, and who knows, perhaps even before that?

Weirdly, if I'm completely honest with myself, I miss the Glome. I'm not meant to miss it, am I? It's not a good thing. It's evil in every way. It poisons everything. Its malevolence infected every part of my life. I know it now. It caused such harm. Perhaps it chose the horrible life I led for me? How could I miss the Glome? What's wrong with me?

I don't want *him* to hear my thoughts.

Panic envelops me. I need to find a way out.

The room is round and white. No doors, only panels. I run, bang on them. No sound. There must be a door somewhere. I just need to find it.

My mind races. How did we get in here? What a ridiculous question. Of course, we used a door. How else would we have entered? But I'm not sure now. Did we use a door? I don't remember.

He catches me, holds me. Though the fear is still inside me, I'm at once calmer, as though his energy mingles with mine, strengthens and stills me.

I hear his voice in my head.

"You're safe now, Lee. Nothing will harm you here. We're here to help you."

I realise he's previously used the plural "we". I wonder what he means, as it's just us here - him and me. Perhaps he's referring to the figures I'd seen in my bathroom. God, that feels like another lifetime.

I'd smile if I could. Perhaps I am smiling, but I can't feel it.

It was another lifetime, I remind myself.

The thought pops out of my mind.

"I still don't understand why you're here. We only knew each other for one day. I thought when you die, people who'd known you, who were important in your life, come to meet you. Not near-strangers - no offence."

He lets me go, and we look at each other.

His smile is dazzling.

"Don't get hung up on what you know about dying. I also thought like you, but this is nothing like it. I don't know why these beliefs exist. Where they came from? People with near-death experiences talk about a light at the end of a tunnel and their loved ones waiting for them there. It may be true for people who return to the material world. But once we're separated from our physical bodies, we experience something very different."

"You're not kidding. I didn't know I'd be watching excerpts from my life. Not sure what to make of it."

He places a hand on my arm.

"I know it's disconcerting in the beginning. But you'll get used to it soon, and then you'll discover how amazing life is. It's not what we understand when we're in our physical bodies.

We get too bogged down in the dramas around us to recognise how phenomenal, how special our lives are."

He crosses his arms, his smile blinding again.

"Plus, we have amnesia in our physical bodies for a reason."

I guess I'm shaking my head because his smile broadens, and I'm relieved my actions are coming across because I still feel nothing.

"I don't get this at all. And what is it with the amnesia? What about the free will thing? If that's even true, why would we choose the physical lives we lead? I mean, why would I have chosen such an appalling start to my life?"

I don't wait for his response because the thought reminds me of the Glome again. I glance around, expecting to see it lurking. But we're still alone in the white, round room with the panels. They flicker again as I look at them, and images appear. I'm wondering if they respond to my thoughts and the attention I give them?

Oh, God, don't tell me it's going to be about the darkness.

I don't know if I can take it.

CHAPTER 5

F IFTEEN MAY. MY BIRTHDAY.

Grandmother is at the hospital with Mother. Conor is at school.

Mary has laid out a party table. She's put three different sorts of biscuits on three separate plates. My eyes keep wandering hungrily to the chocolate ones, but Mary said we couldn't have any until Conor came home from school. Mary had asked Grandmother to bring the biscuits and the bottle of fizzy drink that's in the fridge, and she did. Grandmother also brought three blue balloons. They were supposed to be my surprise, but Mary couldn't blow them up, so Conor did it before he went to school this morning. That's why Mary couldn't hide the balloons from me and instead tied them to my chair with a pink ribbon Mother sometimes put in her hair.

I'm still feeling funny from the other day. My body is achy, and I can't stop sleeping. Grandmother told Mary to keep me awake. It's difficult, but I try. Even though none of us told her, Grandmother seems to know what had happened.

Mary washed my face and wet my hair so she could comb it neatly, as Mother always does after bath time. Conor gave me his old jeans. They're slightly too long, and my nappy feel bunched up in them. Mary rolled up the ends, so I don't trip. I feel kind of grown up in them. But they don't feel like me. They feel like Conor. My red T-shirt is a little too small now, but it's clean, and I have a tickly feeling in my tummy. Mary says it's excitement. Probably because of my party.

Grandmother has been staying with us since Mother went to the hospital. So they don't take us away and split us up, she said to someone on the phone. Everything is different now. She watches us all the time and makes food for us. I miss Mary's cheese toasties every day, and I don't like the green stuff Grandmother gives us to eat. I don't think Mary and Conor like it, either. And we're not allowed to watch as much telly anymore.

Grandmother brought pens and colouring-in books, and she makes us sit at the table to do colouring-in. I really like it, and I don't miss the telly at all. But I can tell Mary hates it. She coloured in her nails, instead, pink like Mother's. When Mary had finished her nails, she coloured in her toenails, then mine. Grandmother made Mary take it all off. Mary cried while she and Grandmother scrubbed her nails and toenails. I don't think Grandmother saw my toenails because she didn't make me clean mine. And she looked sad but said nothing when Mary started drawing little hearts and flowers on the wall around her mattress.

But the biggest change is the smell. Grandmother smokes. A lot. And even though she opens the window when she smokes, it doesn't take away the smell of the cigarettes. The stink lingers even when she's not here. It makes my nose runny, and I sneeze a lot. I know Mary minds the smell, too, but it doesn't seem to affect Conor at all. He still has his routine of doing his homework the moment he's back from school, then getting changed and, when Grandmother isn't here, having cheese toasties while watching the telly. Except, Grandmother doesn't allow him to watch as much as before. She has jobs for him to do before dinner. And we always have dinner at the table together, now. Grandmother sits in Mother's chair.

Mary said we didn't have to wait for Grandmother to have the party. She won't be home until late. I'm happy about it. It means no stinky cigarette smell at my party.

Mary and I are sitting on the sofa watching the telly. She's holding my hand. I'm so sleepy, but she squeezes my hand every time I doze off, and it wakes me up again.

Finally, when I can hardly stand it anymore, Conor buzzes the door code, and Mary goes to let him inside. I go to sit in my chair at the table.

Conor doesn't do his homework immediately today. He gets changed and brings the fizzy drink from the fridge instead. Mary brings three mugs, and they take their seats at the table. Conor pours the fizzy drink for each of us. Then, he slides a small red truck across the table towards me. He must have had it in his pocket. He says nothing, but his eyes are smiling and twinkly. Mary claps her hands and laughs out loud.

I love my little truck at once. I clamber down my chair to give Conor a hug. He smells like outside and like Conor. He smiles and pats my back and head.

I return to my chair, and Conor raises his cup as we've often seen Mother do. Mary and I raise our cups, too. Then, I drink some of the fizzy stuff. It's better than anything I've ever tasted before, and I take a big gulp. But it goes down my nose, and I cough and splutter. I can feel my face and neck going red as I try to breathe.

Conor gets to me quickly. He holds up my arms with one hand and slaps me on the back with the other. It hurts. My back is still sore from the other day. But finally, I can breathe again.

Mary is standing next to me, and she's holding out a small piece of toilet paper so I can wipe my nose. Mother's shown us how to use just one segment of toilet paper, so it lasts longer.

Conor and Mary go back to their chairs, and we eat the biscuits and drink the fizzy drink. Except now, I take only small sips. I laugh because it feels such fun.

Afterwards, while I'm playing with my little red truck, Conor and Mary clear up and clean the party things, and then Conor sits at the table to do his homework.

Mary is in the bedroom, no doubt adding more hearts and flowers to her "mural," as Grandmother calls it.

The door buzzer goes, but we don't answer it. We know it's not Grandmother. Grandmother has a key. We stay quiet. But someone hammers on our door because a neighbour must have opened the big front door. They bang really hard. Mary runs into the living room. She's scared.

I pick up my truck, and we sit on the sofa. Mary holds my hand again, but this time it's for her and not because I need it.

Conor goes to the door.

We can hear his voice.

"Who is it?" he asks, as Mother has taught us.

"Police. Open the door."

Two enormous policemen come into the room.

"Where's your mummy?" one of them asks.

Conor tells them she's at the hospital. They squat down beside us. One of them asks to see the little red truck I'm still holding in my hand.

"That's a lovely truck. Where did you get it?"

Mary tells them it's my birthday today, and it's a present, my first ever toy, from Conor.

The policemen glance at each other, then at Conor. His head is down. He doesn't look at them but his face goes bright red. Then he turns and runs down the hallway to the bedroom.

M OTHER IS HOME.

It feels like she's been away for months and months. Mary had her birthday in July and Conor's was in October, and Mother has been away for both, and mine in May.

All the neighbours came out to watch Mother come home in the ambulance. They cleared a path as the paramedics brought her in a wheelchair. Now, she's sitting on the sofa. She's thin and pale. Her big blue eyes are dark, with black circles underneath. When she moves, it's slow, as though she's in pain. But she's home.

Grandmother is still staying with us. She sleeps in the living room, on the sofa. The room stinks even more of cigarette smoke. Because it's cold - nearly Christmas - Grandmother doesn't always open the window anymore when she's smoking.

Mother sits in the living room for a short time in the morning, near the heater. She wears a thick gown and one of her blankets around her. Grandmother brings Mother tea that she sips a little at a time, like the birds outside the window when they drink the water from the saucer Mary puts there for them.

As soon as Mother has finished her tea, Grandmother helps her to the bathroom to have her bath. I've never seen Mother have a bath before, and now she has one every day. But it exhausts her, and she sleeps almost the whole day afterwards, only waking up when Grandmother gives Mother the medication that came with her from the hospital.

Grandmother never screams or yells at Mother anymore. Mary and I must be even quieter.

But three new things happened.

Conor showed me how to go to the toilet on my own, and now I wear a nappy only at night. But Grandmother says soon I won't need those anymore, either, because I'm a big boy now.

The other momentous thing is that Grandmother takes us to the park every day. We didn't know there was a park. We can even see our flat from the park. There are swings and a sandpit, a seesaw and other children.

At first, Mary and I just sat on the bench with Grandmother while she smoked her cigarettes. I think Mother asked her to take us because of the smell in our home.

It's freezing, and we got a coat each. Mary's is red and mine a deep blue, and we got mittens and woollen hats, too. I think they were meant to be Christmas presents, but we got them early to go to the park. When we breathe out, we can see our breath. It looks a little like Grandmother's smoke, so we pretend to smoke as well, with tiny sticks we find on the ground.

The trees are bare, and I like their dark shapes against the grey sky. I would like to draw them. But Mary wants to play on the swings and the seesaw. She met another girl, also with a red coat. They even look a little alike, with their dark curls bouncing as they run. I like to watch the two red coats as they run here and there, playing tag or just running for the fun of it.

Mary's eyes are bright when we go home, and her cheeks are almost as red as her coat. But we must take off our coats, mittens and hats, and we must stay quiet.

Mary still likes to watch cartoons, and Grandmother lets her, but I love my colouring-in books, and Mary has given me hers, as well. I sit at the table to work.

When Conor comes home from school, he sits opposite me to do his homework, and I continue with my colouring. It feels like we're doing something together. But Conor wears a frown as he works and never looks up at me. I don't mind. Just being with him like this feels good.

The other thing happened when we got to the park today. Grandmother said she was just nipping to the shops and that we could play with our new friends until she came back. She said she wouldn't be long.

I don't think she realised only Mary had a new friend. I watched Mary and her friend running and playing on the seesaw. The friend's mother followed behind them, absorbed in a conversation on her phone. I don't think she even saw me or knew Mary and I were related.

No one saw the man who came to sit next to me on the bench. At first, he just watched Mary and her friend, and her friend's mum. He ate sweets from a brightly coloured packet, turned to offer me one. They looked lovely. The one I took tasted as great as I thought it would. He asked my name, and I told him, Lee. Then he wanted to know how old I was, and I told him, three. He moved closer and said if we sat close together, we wouldn't be so cold. I believed him because Conor said the same thing, and the three of us often slept together for warmth when it was freezing.

I don't know what happened after that. Mary told me later when Grandmother returned with her shopping, I was lying on the wet grass and mud in front of the bench. My body was rigid. Foam bubbled from my mouth, and my eyes rolled back in my head. Mary said that's what Grandmother told the paramedics.

A little distance from our bench, they found a man who'd died, probably from a heart attack. Another ambulance came to collect the man.

It was how Uncle had died, Grandmother said, and the reminder made her sad again, but not for long because she felt guilty for leaving us. I could see it in her eyes.

Mother and I have been to the hospital, and we both have medications to take every day for the rest of our lives, the doctor said. But I didn't have to stay in the hospital, like Mother. And when I got home, Mother seemed pleased when Grandmother told her the doctor said I had epilepsy.

"Like his father," Mother said.

CHAPTER 6

I'M STANDING IN MY new school uniform. I say new, but it's Conor's old one. The uniform is slightly too big. Grandmother says I'll grow into it.

I'm not sure I'll like school, but it has to be better than being home without Conor and Mary.

Mary loves school. She started last year.

Mother said she was much better by then, nearly back to normal, but I wasn't so sure. Mother took Mary to school on her first day, but Mother may as well not have gone because Mary didn't need her. When they arrived at the school gate, Mary ran off to meet her new classmates, leaving Mother to stand alone.

Mother came home later, crying.

Conor took Mary to school and home again every day from then on.

It's silent without Conor and Mary.

Mother is quiet. I'm quiet.

Grandmother left. She said we didn't need her anymore, so she returned home. She still comes by once a week with the shopping, but she never stays long and no longer helps us with bath time. Gradually, her stinky cigarette smell left, too.

I sit at the table and do my colouring every day. We never go to the park anymore. I don't think it would be fun with just Mother and me, anyway.

Grandmother brings more colouring-in books, pens, and some blank books, and I discover I like to draw things. Anything - fruit, the chair, the room, the window, Mother...

Mother sits on the sofa. I think she's watching the telly. But I realise more and more whenever I glance at her, she isn't looking at the screen. She's staring at me. She says nothing. She just stares. At first, not in a bad way. I'd smile at her, and she'd smile back. Then, I'd go back to my colouring or my drawing.

I felt Mother's eyes change gradually as she stared at me.

One day, I looked up, and she looked so scary, I screamed and screamed. I couldn't help myself.

She didn't move, didn't get up to comfort me. Instead, she just smiled, but the smile scared me even more.

I don't remember ever crying like that. I stumbled from the chair and ran into the bedroom, tears streaming down my face, snot dangling from my nose.

Shutting the door, I jumped on my mattress furthest from Mother's bed, pulling my sheets and blankets over my head. My heart was pounding, and my ears had a funny ringing sound.

I was so afraid ugly Mother would come to get me. But nothing happened. Not then.

From that day on, I took my books, pens and things, and did my colouring and drawing on my mattress. I stayed in the bedroom until Conor and Mary came home from school, when my tummy rumbled so loudly from hunger that I wondered if the neighbours could hear it.

Now, Mother always looks at me funny, especially when Conor and Mary are at school, but even sometimes when they're home, just not when they're in the room.

I try to avoid being alone with Mother, but it isn't always possible. And she seems to get me by myself whenever she can. Then she stares at me with her scary eyes.

Her Mother eyes, her kind eyes, are nearly entirely gone. Just glimpses, now and then, remind me of Mother. She has otherwise become a stranger.

If not for Grandmother, who brings food and groceries, or for Conor and Mary, who look after me and seem far older than Mother, somehow, I can't imagine what would have become of me in Mother's care.

No one else seemed to notice the change in her.

One day, I could hear Mother in the bathroom. I sneaked out of the bedroom to get water and crept up the hallway towards the kitchen, but stopped when I reached the closed bathroom door.

I could hear Mother's voice. She was talking to someone in there. But who? We were alone in the flat, and I didn't hear the buzzer or the front door opening. It sounded like two voices - Mother's and a deeper voice that sounded very like Mother's.

It seemed they were arguing.

"Evil, evil child. Do something."

"What? What can I do?"

"He can't take over your brain. No, we won't allow it. We have to end it before he gets too strong. You should never have had him. We told you not to, didn't we?"

"Yes, you did."

"We said something was wrong. But would you listen? Oh, no, of course not. You thought you knew better than us. But you didn't, did you? You knew nothing. And now, this. You're responsible."

"No, I'm not. It's Sean's fault. He did it."

"No, you brought this evil into the world. This thing will grow stronger in that boy and destroy everything in its path."

"But he's a part of me and a part of Sean. We're not evil."

"Ah, but look what it did to Sean, to its own father. Why do you think you would escape?"

"I don't know what to do. I don't know what to do. I don't know what to do."

Mother is repeating the phrase over and over, faster and faster.

Then, silence.

I didn't know what to do. Was Mother in trouble? Suddenly, she was screaming and yelling. Then, an almighty crash.

I sprinted back to the bedroom, shut the door and crawled underneath Mother's bed. My body felt icy all over, and I couldn't stop shaking and panting. I told myself that the queasy feeling in my tummy was probably from hunger and thirst. But when my body shook uncontrollably, I recognised the beginnings of a fit. My legs and arms went rigid, there was a rushing sound in my ears, and I felt the darkness waiting to swallow me, but I was also aware of the silence in the flat.

Just as the darkness tried to take me, I noticed Mother kneeling on the floor beside her bed. Her right hand held back her hair as she peered at me under the bed, her left hand stretched out towards me.

The powerful, dark wrong thing in me I'd named the Glome wanted to come out. It wanted to protect me from Mother, just as it had protected me, Conor and Mary from Uncle and got rid of that horrid man in the park. But I fought it. Pushed it back. I pushed it hard until my entire body was drenched and shaking from the effort.

I screamed at it in my head.

"She's my mother!"

MOTHER CAN'T TAKE ME to school today. Grandmother and Conor and Mary are taking me on my first day.

Mother is in the hospital again. The turn she had has a name - schizophrenia.

Grandmother was calm about it, but seemed surprised. She had a faraway look when she said how odd that both her son and daughter should have it when everyone else in the family was so normal.

CHAPTER 7

I T'S QUIET IN THE flat. And dark.

I guess it must be after midnight because the telly is off, and I can't see the faint strip of light seeping under the bedroom door from the living room.

Only Mary and I still sleep in Mother's bedroom. Conor has been sleeping in the living room for a while now.

Mother put Conor's mattress up against the wall, which has helped keep down the noise from the next-door neighbours. There's a darker blue patch on the carpet where Conor's mattress was. Only Mary's and my mattresses are still on the floor, but we have more space now.

I'm aware of Mary and Mother's presence in the room and their soothing, rhythmic breathing. Why am I awake when everyone else is asleep? I'm not sure what woke me up, but whatever it was, it's gone now.

I yawn.

A wonderful sense of contentment washes over me. My life is perfect.

Conor and Mary finally saw Mother was heading for another turn. They told Grandmother, and she took Mother back to the hospital. They adjusted her medication, and I'm so happy Mother is back to her beautiful self again. She still sometimes has a turn, but it's the other kind when empty bottles are in the living room. But even that doesn't happen very often anymore.

Mother has a job now. It's only part-time at the charity shop down the road. I don't think she likes it much, but Grandmother says it's good for her. She gets to meet other people there, and she's out of the flat until we come home.

It's nice that we all come back at the same time every day. I like it very much.

Even school isn't as bad as I once feared. It was difficult in the beginning. There was that time when Conor hit the bigger boy's nose because he and another boy were throwing my schoolbag at each other. I tried to catch it, but they threw it over my head and laughed when I couldn't reach it. Conor saw what was happening as he approached our class to collect me. He said nothing. He just hit the guy on the nose. That stopped their silly little game.

And the other time, Mary yanked that girl's ponytail because she grabbed the sandwiches Mary had packed for my lunch.

The girl thought it was hilarious when I started crying. A group of girls stood around her, and she kept saying, "Little piggie, come and get your sarnies."

Mary came round the corner to have lunch with me, as she did once a week. Mary knew everyone and shouted the girl's name, but the girl was too busy taunting me to hear Mary. So, Mary yanked her by the ponytail until she let go of my sandwiches.

After that, no one paid me much attention, good or bad.

But when art classes started and everyone saw my drawings, their attitude towards me changed completely. Everyone said my voice was extraordinary when I was accepted to sing in the choir.

I'm not in anyone's clique, but no one excludes me. I can go wherever and talk to whomever I want, but I seldom do so.

Somehow, I don't know how, I suspect from Mary, Grandmother heard about the troubles at school. Grandmother told Mother we should all move to Liverpool, where other family members lived and where we could get a bigger place so that she could come to live with us and help.

Mother said she didn't think it was a good idea. But I think it became Grandmother's mission in life to get us to Liverpool. Especially after Mother, in the grip of one of her rare exhilarated turns, gave us baked beans and eggs for breakfast one day, and I shat my pants in class.

Conor had to bring me home and help me clean myself. He missed an important maths test that day. Conor is clever, and so is Mary, and I have my art and my voice.

Grandmother was furious that Conor had missed his maths test.

"You don't realise how important these tests are to his future," Grandmother told Mother. "You want him to have a better future, don't you?"

Mother said nothing. She looked like me when the teacher scolded me, head down, eyes on the floor, fingers intertwined.

I'm still thinking about school and my perfect life when I suddenly know exactly what woke me.

It was a voice. Was the voice inside my head? It sounded very near. That's why I assumed it was inside my head. Now I think about it, it was definitely in my right ear. I'm sure of it.

It was a man's voice saying my name. A very gentle sound, like a feather being drawn over my ear.

"Lee," it said.

It wasn't a question or statement. It was just the voice saying my name.

I lie in the dark, my eyes and ears stretched to their limits as I wait for the voice to speak again, say something more, or even repeat my name. I need to know it wasn't my imagination. But already, I knew it was real.

I MUST HAVE DRIFTED off to sleep again because I wake up when Mary and Mother move around, getting ready for school and work.

I don't know whether to feel relieved I didn't hear the voice again. Perhaps it was just my imagination after all, or more likely, it was a dream.

I say nothing, but at breakfast, even Conor comments that I'm unusually quiet. Mary and Mother both cast enquiring glances my way.

On the way to school, we wait, as usual, at the busy intersection for the traffic lights to change. When the pedestrian green light comes on, we walk amid a crowd to the other side of the road.

Just as we reach the centre of the big intersection, I hear the voice again. It's very clear but urgent, even though it's soothing. It's close to my right ear, so close that I turn to see who's speaking to me. But no one's there. Everyone around me is talking to whoever they're with or busy crossing the street in silence, their thoughts their only companions.

The voice repeats my name. It isn't part of the sounds I hear around me. It's too clear and near, coming from somewhere too quiet, like some other realm. But this time, even though it's still measured and calm, it's more urgent. I know with absolute certainty it's a warning to get off the road. At once.

My heart beats in my throat. I can feel the adrenaline coursing through my body. I grab Conor and Mary's hands and pull them to walk faster. They complain and resist.

Moments later, the truck comes. A huge lorry. One of those with many wheels, from the Continent. It careers out of control towards the people around us and us. It's chaos. People are screaming and running in all directions. Cars are hooting and trying to avoid crashing into each other, people and the oncoming truck.

Conor and Mary no longer resist or complain. They're pulling me now. We run as fast as we can to get away from the lorry. It is difficult to move through the crowd. There are so many people, and everyone's panicking.

The overwhelming stench of burnt rubber follows plumes of dark white smoke. I gag as it hits the back of my throat. My eyes are streaming, and I know the tears are not only from crying. The sounds of brakes screeching on the road assault my ears. But the massive truck's momentum drives it into the crowd.

I can hear people's bones crush and break. The sickening thudding sound of the truck driving over cars, bodies, and bags makes my loud voice scream in panic. Mary and I are sobbing, but Conor is silent, his face white. We're running as fast as we can.

Behind us, the truck is still moving. The many cars and bodies it crashed into have slowed it. It comes to a thundering halt when it hits the traffic pole to our right.

We reach the opposite side of the road and stop. Mary and I are bent over, gulping air. Conor stands, nostrils flared, hands on hips, staring at the carnage in the road.

People from the shops are outside on the pavement. They make a fuss of us, steering us away from the horror, offering to call Mother, offering tea with sugar for the shock.

We allow them to take us away. Only Conor glances behind him as we're led into the greasy spoon cafe. We're offered tea, and a large woman with a massive bosom stays with us, her hands warm on my shoulders.

She doesn't talk to us but shouts instructions to others. Now and then, she gives us a kind, toothy smile.

"Don't worry, my lovelies. You're safe now."

The shrill sounds of ambulances and police cars announce their imminent arrival.

A few other casualties also sit at the Formica tables. They're silent, mugs of steaming sweet tea in front of them, shocked expressions in their eyes, smudges of dirt on their clothes and pale faces, hair a mess.

Someone must have called Mother. She comes running through the door and nearly sags to the floor with relief when she sees us.

The woman with the big bosom hugs Mother and then leaves to bring another mug of sweet tea. Mother cries and embraces each of us for a long time. Then she sits down at the table with us and drinks her tea.

We don't have to go to school. Mother doesn't go back to work, either. We stay in the greasy spoon cafe until the police take our statements. Then, Mother walks home with us, but we take a different route.

Grandmother comes around. She brings food and fizzy drinks and sits with us the whole afternoon. We watch the accident on the telly.

CHAPTER 8

I TURN AWAY FROM the screens as the images fade and the panels revert to blank whiteness.

He's still here.

How odd. I could taste his name on my tongue all this time, but only have it pop into my mind now.

James...

It's a good, solid name that feels like the person bearing that name would be considerate, warm and kind. Indeed, all the things I experienced from James when we were alive

But I shouldn't be surprised at those thoughts. I've always been interested in names and their meanings, probably because of my Celtic roots and my mother's obsession with names.

She chose a good name for me - Lee. I've always liked it, but it means healer, and I've never felt remotely like one. Which reminds me - I'm sure I've read somewhere that the name James means changeling. And this James has undoubtedly changed. I sense his playful energy still emanating from him, but it's been supplanted by something far more profound. I wish I had a name for it.

He's watching me, and I realise he was right earlier when he said I'd get used to all this soon. I'm certainly not as upset about seeing my life play out like a movie anymore. I'm not even that concerned about the darkness anymore. Didn't I just see the Glome wasn't all bad? It protected me and Mary, and Conor. It must have had a purpose.

But things from that life seem to recede from me the longer I'm here, wherever here is, away from the life I once knew. Well, at least I think I'm okay about it all now.

I've realised something else. Watching these extracts from my life shows how much I've learned as a spiritual being while in my physical body, even when I imagined none of this while I was alive. Perhaps the physical body and the spiritual one can't really be separated. Isn't it how we feel in the material world? Separated.

I see James's smile out of the corner of my eye.

Perhaps he read my mind or understood I'm questioning, in a new way, the point of our physical lives, the meaning behind it. Clearly, we don't disappear when we die. I'm still here, aren't I? Only my physical body died. Maybe I should be upset about it, but I'm not. I haven't even cried about my body dying yet.

James moves next to me. His eyes stay on mine as his voice appears in my head.

"You're right. When we're in the material world, we take everything there so seriously. But it's not about only being physical, is it? Our focus on our physical lives is due to the fact that we enter that world with no recollection of anything. It's necessary. Otherwise, our spiritual selves cannot evolve and grow into who we're becoming, for we're always becoming eternally. We're never done."

I feel myself nodding. I don't necessarily agree with James because I don't understand some of what he says, but I think it will be revealed.

Something is nagging at the edge of my mind. It's something to do with the amnesia, the cohesion of our spiritual and physical bodies, and the darkness that lived inside me for all my earthly years. But I can't think clearly because the enormous power of light that runs through me and envelops me like a second skin distracts me utterly. I wonder if I feel it so strongly because I'm used to a powerful energy, albeit dark, being such an integral part of my life for so long?

I wonder if James can feel this light, too.

Before I can ask him, the panels around us glow, become transparent, and seem to dissolve as many light forms appear around us. I realise they may have been the light forms that accompanied us here and could have been behind the panels all along. I just couldn't see them until now.

As I watch, fascinated, the beings grow in stature and become many lengths taller than James and me. They're surrounding us, and their light is blinding. My eyes should hurt. But they don't. Instead, I hear the most beautiful sounds emanating from the beings. It's soft and like no other sound I've ever heard – not voices singing, exactly. But that comes closest to what I'm experiencing. The sound is mesmerising, and for moments, I forget where I am. Not that I actually know where I am, I remind myself.

I notice something else. The enormous energy I feel around and inside me appears even stronger when I listen to the sound of the light beings, as though the light and the sound are connected somehow.

As the experience intensifies, I lose myself. An emotion I can only describe as ecstasy takes over my entire being. I turn around and around, trying to drink it in, hold on to it for as long as possible. Unimaginable joy bubble up inside me, and I throw back my head to let it out through the best, most freeing laughter I've ever experienced. I want to scream, dance, and cry, and I never want the feeling to stop.

My eyes are closed, and I sense we're moving again. It's fast. Faster than before.

I want to open my eyes, but James is beside me, his voice in my head.

"Keep your eyes closed. You'll get too disorientated otherwise. You'll get used to it later, I promise."

I trust James, so I keep my eyes closed and instead focus on the sensation of movement, sound, and energy I'm experiencing.

I still can't get over how free and joyful I am, how the enormous light energy has penetrated all of me, so I feel as though I'm glowing.

We move for ages, and I love every second. I don't want it to stop. But we do.

At first, I don't realise we're no longer moving. My eyes are still closed, and I'm aware of the sound of water nearby.

James's voice is soothing in my head.

"We're here, Lee. You can open your eyes now."

I have no words to describe what I see.

We're in a garden. But it's like no garden I've ever seen, not even on the telly in one of those programmes Grandmother used to love watching. It showed gardens from around the world. She loved the stunning Italian gardens the most.

But this garden has colours so vivid, I blink to make sure they're real. The leaves on the trees are green, but the colour is so intense and displays variations behind the different greens. It leaves me dazed. All around, flowers show similar nuances and hues that make up their primary colours. But everything appears layered and far more intricate than the three-dimensional world I'm used to. Some colours I didn't know existed.

The garden goes on and on, disappearing into the horizon that melds with a sky so blue it seems the ocean is above us.

To my right, a small fountain spews water from an oversized acorn on top of it. But even the fountain displays colours I've never seen before. It's not metal exactly or concrete but something else similar.

Birds sit on the lawn beneath it or on the lip of the fountain. Some bathe in the water that appears to shimmer with an energy that runs through everything here.

And the birds? Oh, my word! Such colours. Such feathers. So beautiful that tears form in my eyes. In my wildest imagination, I could never have painted anything so exquisite.

James steps before me, and I realise he shimmers like everything here.

"Are you ready, Lee?"

"Ready for what?"

James indicates I should walk with him.

In the distance, I see our road as it looked when I was a kid and we still lived in Ireland.

What's it doing here?

Before I ask, James must hear the question in my head.

"This more interactive experience is necessary, Lee. You'll understand it all soon, I promise. Just trust the process."

I want to ask more questions, but I find myself in our flat as though I'm there. But I'm watching myself too. I can move around without my family or physical self seeing me as I am now.

I'm not sure I like this. The panels that showed my life are what I prefer.

CHAPTER 9

A MONTH GOES BY, and Mary and I still regularly wake up screaming from our nightmares about the accident. But I don't hear the voice in my ear anymore.

Mother is angry because Conor has become even more distant and has started smoking. Although he denies it when she confronts him, I can smell it on him, too.

Conor hangs out with his friends after school now. He only comes home later to have dinner by himself.

Grandmother says he's in with the wrong crowd. I don't know how she knows this, but I'm not surprised. Grandmother knows lots of things. But Mother doesn't believe Grandmother and allows Conor to go to the park to meet his friends every day. She says she can't really stop him because everyone's doing it, and she'd rather know where he is.

Mary and I aren't sure Conor is in the park. We've seen him around with older boys. They don't hang out in the park, but we don't tell Mother or Grandmother.

When our nightmares about the accident continue, and Conor comes home later and later, often angry and drunk,

Mother finally agrees with Grandmother. It may be a good idea to move to Liverpool. A fresh start for everyone.

I think her decision is mostly to get Conor away from the bad influence Grandmother talks about every time she comes to visit.

I DIDN'T KNOW MOVING was this exciting.

If I'm honest, I wasn't looking forward to it. I can't imagine myself living anywhere other than in our flat. I can't imagine my mattress in another room.

Mother said when we move, I'll have my own room, with a proper bed and not only a mattress. It sounds scary, but Mary and Conor are both excited about it because Mother said they'll each have their own rooms with beds as well.

Mary has already decided to paint each wall in her room a different colour. By the sounds of it, pinks and purples.

Conor doesn't want to show his excitement, but I can see it shining in his eyes. The only thing he's said out loud is it would be great to have his own privacy.

But I'm not thinking about having my privacy. I don't care about it, though Mary said I'd want it someday soon. Instead, I'm thinking about the new school and making new friends there, and maybe having all the troubles all over again, like when I started at my old school. No one at the new school would know me. They wouldn't understand me. How will I survive? I don't have the energy to start over again.

But the moving machine is rolling along now, and despite my misgivings, I get sucked into the excitement of it. It feels like the run-up to Christmas or someone's birthday or something.

And then, suddenly, moving day is here.

We have little to pack. At least, I do.

But Grandmother has loads, and the truck is almost completely full with her stuff by the time it arrives outside our flat. Grandmother came along with the van. Once Mother lets Grandmother and the men inside, Grandmother organises everyone to get our things into the truck.

Mary and I had our things packed ages ago, just keeping out the clothes for the journey and our toothbrushes till the last moment.

Mary has a small pink suitcase on wheels filled with clothes and books. Her school bag is also bulging with the rest of her belongings.

The black rucksack I'd inherited from Conor has my clothes and books. The rest of my books are in my school bag.

I know Grandmother has bribed Conor with money to get him to pack his stuff and stay home with us, so we can all go to Liverpool together. He's sulking and being as difficult with Mother as he can be, either ignoring her altogether or grunting when she asks him for help. But perhaps because of the promise of more money from Grandmother, eventually, he does what Mother asks before returning to sit on the sofa and staring with non-seeing eyes at something on the telly. Everything gets put inside the back of the truck quickly with the men helping, and soon, much sooner than I want, we're ready to leave.

We walk around for the last time, supposedly to check that nothing is left behind, but I can see we're all, in our own ways, saying goodbye.

Mary goes from room to room, saying, "Goodbye living room, goodbye bathroom, goodbye kitchen..."

Our flat feels bigger, strange, empty, as though we've never lived here at all, as though all the things that happened here were just dreams or stuff I made up in my head, or like they happened to someone else.

The furniture is staying behind, but everything else is coming with us.

Mother's bedroom looks much bigger without our mattresses on the floor. Grandmother organised for them to be taken to the rubbish tip early this morning. Mother's mattress also went there. Her bed, now just a wooden frame, stands naked, small and unimportant. The threadbare carpet is a denser, darker blue where the mattresses used to be near the walls. Their shapes on the carpet are the only signs they were here at all.

We can't travel with the truck. We go on a bus with Mother because there isn't room.

I've never been to the ferry pier before. It's like another world. I kind of knew what to expect, of course, because I'd seen the ferry pier on the news before. But to be here, to see it all for myself, to inhale the salty sea air, and the oil smells from the ferries and to hear the sharp sounds from the seagulls, and the people, some happy, some sad, all this other life around me, is simultaneously wonderful, and terrifying.

Grandmother buys us ice cream from the van with the bright pictures. It plays a tune that gets sharper and hurts my ears when we go closer. But I'm grateful for the ice cream and snatch mine from Grandmother's hand so I can get away from the noise of the van at once. I don't stop to listen to Grandmother's lecture on good manners as I make my way across to the other side and sit down on a wooden bench.

Mary hops and skips to sit beside me, her eyes bright and cheeks red with the excitement of the ice cream and the journey ahead.

Mother walks with Grandmother. They're silent as they lick their ice creams.

If I lean over to the left, I can see Conor chatting to a girl in front of the ice cream van. He's given his ice cream to her. She's licking it but looks like she's crying. Conor has his hands in his jeans pockets, and he's looking down at his shoes, kicking at some small invisible thing. I wonder if the girl is his girlfriend and if he's as sad he's leaving her behind, as she seems to be about him going.

I don't know what I feel.

CHAPTER 10

STRANGERS COME TO MEET us off the ferry, but Grandmother seems to know them. She's excited to see them. They hug and kiss her, then us.

A gigantic man with a big belly and red cheeks, who Grandmother introduces as her brother, pinches my nose and ruffles my hair like I'm a little kid.

Everyone here talks funny, and I listen carefully to understand what they say. But neither Mother and Grandmother nor Conor and Mary seem to have the same problem.

I wonder if they're just pretending.

We're split up. Mother, Mary and Grandmother go with her big brother in his car. A woman who looks like Grandmother – only thinner – and another man - probably her husband - are in a car with us. Both are silent. We sit in the back and look out the windows as we drive.

I'm not comfortable in the car, but Conor seems relaxed, as though he's been in one many times. It's too small, and it doesn't feel the same as travelling on a bus.

Everything here looks dull, and I don't see many trees or parks. Instead, the grey pavements and buildings seem to run seamlessly up into the sky. I get a sense this city is much bigger than our old one.

We drive through a lot of traffic. I'm getting sleepy and lean my head against the window.

I MUST HAVE DRIFTED off because I open my eyes when we pull up to a house on a street where all the houses look the same. But at least each has a tiny patch of grass in front of them, some neatly trimmed, others left to grow in whichever way they see fit.

The car stops, and the woman in the passenger seat opens her door. She smiles at us encouragingly and motions for us to do the same. Grandmother, Mother and Mary are already standing on the pavement in front of a house.

Grandmother's voice reaches me before we get close to them.

"… a lovely house. We'll all be so happy here. Let's get inside."

Mother and Mary follow Grandmother through the small gate hanging off its hinges, along the tiny path with broken bricks to the front door.

I can see by Mother's steps she's not convinced this house is good for us. Her feet move slowly, as though she's reluctant to walk into our new life. I can't blame her. The paintwork is peeling from the bricks, and the front door shows signs of having been painted many times in different colours, one over the other and faded graffiti decorations here and there. Panes are missing from several windows, and cardboard fills the gaps.

The large uncle with the enormous stomach has the keys and pushes past us to open the door. His round face glistens with sweat, and his breathing is loud as he stands aside, allowing Grandmother to enter the house ahead of him.

The stench is the first thing I notice. It's not only musty but also other, older, stinky smells lurk behind the cold, unlived-in air that wafts out, eager to escape into the street.

I notice Conor zipping up his parka and wonder if he's experiencing the same chill I feel, like a foreboding of something terrible waiting for us. I don't want to go inside. But Grandmother walks ahead of us. She claps her hands together as she "oohs" and "ahhs" over the fireplaces in each room and declares them originals, going on about how lucky we are to have these in this house.

She opens windows as she goes from room to room, and I must confess, the air quality improves at once. The place is neglected, but even Mother and Mary are swept up by Grandmother's enthusiasm about cleaning the house and making it lovely and liveable for us.

It doesn't take long to realise there aren't enough bedrooms for us all. Grandmother has made it clear she will live with us. This means Conor and I will have to share a room. He appears to come to the same verdict when I do, and he doesn't seem happy about it. I play along with him, but secretly I'm delighted I won't be sleeping by myself.

As the weeks go by, Grandmother's energy and passion for transforming the house into a home infect us too. Grandmother seems to know a string of workmen with excellent skills. I marvel at how quickly the bathroom and kitchen are transformed into the kind I've only ever seen in Mary's decorating magazines. Even Conor reluctantly, at first, helps to paint the walls in the living room and in our room. True to her promise, Mary insists on painting the walls in her room different shades of pinks and purples. I thought it would be ghastly, but I see how stunning it looks and congratulate her on her vision as she finishes each wall.

Every day, Grandmother makes Mother help her in the garden. As the days go by, the transformation in Mother is extraordinary. I always thought she was pretty, but now she is beautiful. Her eyes sparkle, her skin glows, her hair bounces as she walks, and she smiles all the time. Her voice is kind and soft even though her hands are rough from working in the soil.

I'm amazed every day this is how ordinary people live. Our old life was far from normal, and I am thankful for this new one. But there's one thing that mars the joy I feel. I cross off the days on the calendar in the kitchen with trepidation about the start of the new school year.

The kerfuffle of getting new school uniforms and my haircut fills me with dread for what awaits me. When the day arrives, and Grandmother and Mother go with the three of us to the new school, I try to remember to keep breathing. But the first day is okay. Conor and Mary seem to fit in just as I'd expected. I'm grateful for the art classes and the choir, which again makes me feel less than a freak. I keep my head down but can already feel the animosity when people look at me, so I'm not surprised when a group of girls mock me as I walk past them.

"Look at the lard-arse on that," one of them says.

"Miss Ogilvy is out of her mind if she thinks this idiot can replace Mark's solo parts in the choir," another voice says.

"You've got to be kidding...," yet another exclaims.

I walk away as fast as possible, but my face is burning, and tears sting my eyes. What the hell is it that people dislike about me?

But I know, don't I? It's the darkness, the Glome. Even if they can't see it, somehow, everyone can feel it.

Remembering the Glome and the powerful feeling it always brings makes me lift my chin, straighten my shoulders and slow my steps.

I slow even more as I turn the corner and see several guys hanging out at the massive tree near the gate. They're older, and no one need tell me they're the rebels, the bad boys. None are wearing ties. Shirts hang over their trousers, and they wear white sneakers instead of black school shoes. One of them even flaunts a messy man-bun, which I'm sure is a no-no.

A group of girls has gathered near the gate, and it's easy to see they're pretending not to ogle the rebels. But the girls' too-loud voices and hysterical laughter give them away.

There's no other way I know out of the schoolyard. I must go through the gate and brace myself as I near it. The man-bun guy pushes himself away from the tree and walks towards me. He must be their leader, I reckon.

Here we go. I ready myself for the trouble I'm sure is coming, breathing out slowly through my mouth.

I'm surprised the guy's smiling at me. He clasps an arm around my shoulders and walks me towards his group.

"Hey man, you're that new kid from Ireland, Lee. Am I right?"

I nod but don't look at any of them, preferring to keep my eyes on the ground.

The man-bun guy tells me he's Ned, then introduces each one of his friends, all the while keeping his arm around my shoulders.

I'm unsure what it means, so I nod and say "Hi."

Ned tells me they're on their way to the corner shop for some nibbles and suggests I go with them.

I shrug to show it's okay.

I'm not expected home at a specific time, and I'm sure Grandmother and Mother would both be relieved to know I can make friends like Conor and Mary.

As we near the shop, Ned pulls me aside.

"None of us actually have any money, Lee, mate. So, you need to stay by the door and make sure the security doesn't stop us when we grab the stuff and run. Think you can do that?"

I'm a little surprised. It's not what I expected Ned would ask of me, but perhaps that's how things are done here.

"Sure."

I heave my rucksack further onto my shoulder and wait by the door. Should have asked Ned to get my favourite chocolate biscuits as I'm a little hungry myself.

Ned and the guys run out of the shop not long after entering it. They'd shoved stuff inside their clothes, and a few packets fall to the floor as they run past me. I try to follow, but they're too fast.

Strong hands grab my shoulders from behind. I know it's the store's security guard, but I'm not scared. The man swings me around to face him. He's huge, with a shaven head and tattoos on his neck, which I'm pretty sure goes down both arms.

His voice starts as a low growl and rises to a crescendo.

"Where are you going, you little prick? Come here!"

He tries to drag me back to the shop, but I plant my feet firmly on the pavement. After all, I haven't done anything wrong, and my weight helps a little too.

That's when I hear the voice again.

"Lee," it says close to my right ear. It sounds so calm and like it's from another, quieter place.

I see the guard lifting his arm. Something glints in his hand as he brings it down towards my head. But the Glome stirs, peers at the man, and pushes so hard that he falls. His head smack against the pavement reverberates through my feet and legs.

I turn and run home as fast as possible, my rucksack bouncing on my back.

CHAPTER 11

GRANDMOTHER'S HANDS ARE IN fists on her hips, and her face is like thunder, looking for a place to vent her fury. She says it's the third time the police have knocked on her door in her life.

I knew she meant the time Uncle had died and then again when Conor stole the little red truck for my birthday, and now, obviously. But the way Mother looks at her as Grandmother says it makes me wonder if she's lying.

The two policemen decline coffee and seats, preferring to stand, coming to the point at once, saying they'd seen the CCTV footage of me at the shop. I didn't appear to have stolen anything, but they wanted to know if I was part of the gang that did.

I guess they're trying to get me to give them Ned and his friends' names. But my life at school will be even more difficult if I do, so I pretend not to know who they're talking about. Instead, I say it must have been a coincidence I was there at the same time as the gang. But I can see the officers don't believe me, and I remember Ned's arm around my shoulders as we walked towards the shop. I wonder if the CCTV camera caught it?

Grandmother intervenes when the policemen ask how I'd shoved the security guard so hard that he'd injured his head and had to be taken to the hospital.

Grandmother stands, eyes narrowed as she glares at the two officers.

"Oh, how ridiculous. I'm assuming the security guard was not only an adult but probably a big man. How on earth could a scrawny twelve-year-old child shove him so hard that he injures his head?"

The officers share a meaningful glance, but I can see there's nothing else they can do.

I'm certainly not going to tell them about the Glome. I'm not that stupid. And no one would believe me anyway if I did. My family, who lives with me and knows me, doesn't even know about the Glome, and he's right here with us the whole time.

WHEN I GET TO school the next day, I appreciate how wise my decision was not to grass on Ned and the guys.

The entire school sits in silence in assembly as the headteacher leads the officers and Ned and his mates to his office.

I was worried when they didn't ask me to go with them because Ned glares at me as he walks past, clearly blaming me for the police having found them.

But when they return half an hour later, Ned winks at me and a tiny smile curls around his mouth. I knew he understood

I had nothing to do with it. The police must have tracked them down because of the small identifiers on their uniforms.

I can see the determination in Ned's eyes. They'd be wiser and more careful about CCTV in the future.

I can't help leaning back in my chair and sighing silently through my lips. Until that moment, I didn't realise how tense my body was.

It's even more surprising and satisfying that several girls who clearly admire Ned and his friends turn their attention on me, albeit momentarily. They must have seen him winking at me. But Wendy Jones stares at me with her beautiful chocolate eyes, as though she's only just noticed me.

Almost daily now, every teacher is talking about the end-of-year dance.

Conor is quiet about it, and I wonder if he still misses his girlfriend in Ireland. But he's popular with girls here despite his standoffishness, or perhaps because of it.

Mary's uber-excited about the dance. She can't stop talking about it and hinting she'd need a "special dress." She's also popular with the boys, though I don't think she has a boyfriend.

Grandmother and Mother both say how lucky we are to have such things offered to us and how nice it must be because neither of them had attended end-of-year dances at their schools. I guess they didn't have them in Grandmother's day, and Mother says she was ill when hers happened. She says we're lucky our school offers it every year to every age group because she only had that one chance and missed it.

But to be honest, I'm dreading it. I know no one would want to go with me, and I've already started creating a list of excuses for why I won't be going. Now, with the girls noticing me and perhaps Ned's help, I might be allowed to go.

A tiny butterfly dares to flitter in my stomach at the thought, and Wendy Jones's dark eyes.

—————ℓℓℓ—————

A T THE END OF the school day, I'm not surprised to find Ned and friends waiting for me near the gate. I slow down as I walk towards them, unsure of what to expect. But one thing I know for certain - I don't want to be their lookout for another shop robbery again.

On the other side of the gate, the group of girls has gathered as though they can't tear themselves away from the bad boys. They sound like hens though they're all beautiful, especially Wendy Jones.

As before, Ned walks towards me and puts an arm around my shoulders, steering me towards his friends.

"Lee, man, you were awesome. Not only did you get that security guard away from us, but you didn't grass us up to the coppers."

He claps my back, and the rest of the gang follows his example. I cough as the slaps get a little boisterous.

Ned's grin seems sincere as he looks into my eyes.

"You're an honorary member of the Rooks now. It's what we call ourselves when we don't want anyone to know our plans."

I feel myself swallow, and my voice sounds far away when I speak, getting weaker at the end of my sentence.

"You've got plans?"

I really don't want to be a part of their plans or gang. But I guess I'm already involved, no matter my feelings about it.

The guys laugh, and Ned slaps me on my back again.

"Do we have plans? Oh, Lee, if only you knew. We've got plans, and you'll be one of us all the way."

I think he means it as a good thing. But I want to run away, crawl under my bed and never be found again. I don't know what I want to do with my life, but crime hadn't crossed my mind, and it's clear to me now, this is where these guys are heading.

Damn! My brain can't work fast enough, and I can't think of a single reason for not joining them. Instead, I nod, sigh and shuffle my feet.

Ned ruffles my hair.

"Great Lee, mate. We're in for a crazy good time. You'll see."

The girls are laughing and being too loud again.

Ned must have caught my glance at Wendy. He turns to whisper in my ear.

"You like her, don't you? Want me to set you guys up for the dance?"

My face is on fire, and I lean forward, my eyes on my shoes to hide it. But before I can compose myself and stop Ned, he lets go of me, and I know, by their squeals, he's approaching the girls.

A sudden silence and murmuring tell me he's talking to Wendy, but the roar in my ears is so loud, I can't hear his words.

I shouldn't have been shocked, but the laughter that follows is incredulous, mocking, humiliating.

I don't wait. Running through the gate as fast as I can, I don't care that my rucksack is banging painfully on my back, and my breath is rasping in my throat through the tears that blind me. Before I'm forced to stop, I run as long as I can. I'm not athletic, and the adrenaline only helps so far.

I notice I'm in a lane I don't recognise. There are trees here and a bench. I sink down on it, elbows on my thighs, head in my hands as I try to control my sobs and breathing. I have a stitch in my side from running which doesn't help.

What the hell?

Why do things always go so wrong for me? I can't rid myself of the humiliation and rejection that sit inside my heart like a bunch of stones.

Mary showed me how to slow my breathing and I try to remember to breathe low in my belly for five counts, hold for five, breathe out for five, hold for five. I do this five times, keeping count with my fingers. It works a little and I try to think of something nice, just like Mary had suggested. I think of my art and my singing. But that doesn't bring the relief I crave, either.

Even though things had started off well with the teachers and my classmates liking my artwork, it soon became clear that jealousy had reared its ugly head. One day, I got to art class, and the piece I'd been working on had been destroyed. From then on, it happened in every class. I tried to adapt to it and eventually started taking my art home. Then the brushes and paints weren't enough, so I was left with nothing.

A similar scenario happened with the choir. Mark is apparently much loved among students and teachers alike. It was easy to see how people defended him against the "enemy" they found in my voice. First, I was relegated to the baritones because I was too tall for the tenors, and I blocked the baritones behind me. Then, I was asked to watch instead of sing because my lyric tenor voice couldn't reach some of the baritone notes, which spoiled the harmonies. And now this.

Why couldn't Ned just leave it out?

When I can breathe again without feeling the stitch in my side, I sigh, get up and walk to the end of the lane so I can get my bearings for home. But just as I turn the corner, I'm surprised to see Wendy standing by herself, waiting for a bus at the bus stop. I want to turn around, but she's spotted me and waves. I don't want to be rude, so I wave back and walk towards her.

As I get nearer, I notice her eyes and the tip of her nose are red, like she's been crying. She has a tissue in her hand, suggesting she's been upset. I hope Ned hasn't said anything to make her this sad. Bloody Ned. Why couldn't he leave things alone?

I can't help myself and put my hand on her arm.

"Are you okay?"

Wendy's beautiful eyes swim with tears, and I draw her to me, holding her gently as she rests her head against me. It's how I soothe Mary when life gets too much, so this should feel comfortable, but my heart is pounding, and my breathing is fast and high in my chest.

Wendy's body is small, soft and unfamiliar, and she's shivering like the tiny bird we once rescued from the rain before the Glome snapped its neck.

But Mary's vulnerability does things to me, and I want to squeeze her tighter, kiss her lovely lips, protect her.

Behind me, quick footsteps appear and a male voice growls.

"What the fuck are you doing? Get away from her. She's my girlfriend, you lard-arse."

Wendy's shivering against my chest increases at the sound of the voice, and she shakes her head, showing he's lying.

For moments I almost smile with relief that Mary's distress has nothing to do with Ned or me.

I don't look around as my voice responds without a thought from me, surprising us all.

"She's upset, and you're probably the reason. I'm soothing her. Or are you too stupid to see it?"

There's a moment's shocked silence before the voice growls again.

"Are you deaf? I said get away from my girlfriend."

Strong hands grab me from behind and twist me around. Wendy is spun away from me and falls to the ground with a cry.

I go to help her up, but a searing pain flashes across my left cheek. Out of the corner of my eye, I see two things simultaneously, a knife glinting in the late sun and blood dripping on my white shirt.

Grandmother's going to kill me.

CHAPTER 12

M Y HEAD IS IN my hands as I try to blank the scene from my eyes, but I'm aware I'm once again in the extraordinary other-worldly garden with James.

There are no flickering lights this time. There's just the jolt from that reality to this one. I feel dizzy, as though I've been on a merry-go-round.

"What the hell was that?"

I meant to ask out loud, but James must have heard my thought.

"You're ready for some answers, Lee. Follow me."

James walks ahead of me along a path laid in stunning stones that shimmer with the same strange energy that permeates everything here. It captures my attention for a moment. But as I look up, I see we're approaching a colossal white building. Myriad colours run through the white, turning it into a rainbow mirage.

I follow James up many steps towards the gigantic white door that swings open as we get closer and we find ourselves in a long, broad corridor with another oversized entrance at the end. As we approach it, James stands aside for me to enter first.

I'm not sure what I expected, but I'm stunned by the vast space. We're in a theatre with a stage and a single row of seats surrounding it. People are already sitting in the chairs as though they've been waiting for us. They also have the weird but beautiful energy flowing through near-diaphonous bodies. I feel I should know them but don't recognise anyone. They're a mixed bunch-some are children. But I understand their appearance has very little to do with the energy of immense wisdom that flows from them in streams I can almost see and touch. Everyone is dressed in the same flowing white robes James and I wear.

James leads me to the middle of the stage and swipes his hand in the air. A gigantic hologram appears. The scene is the same as where we are now, so it seems we're watching ourselves, watching ourselves, watching ourselves, in an infinite loop. I've seen similar things in films and briefly wonder if this is their version of such a movie. But I know it's "real," whatever that means, because I'm watching myself standing on the stage.

As I look at the image on the hologram, a swirling white fog appears and mercifully obscures the pictures that are doing my head in. In their place, only one image appears in the mist. But it's more than an image and reminds me of my recent experience viewing my life – being there but unseen.

I look to James for an explanation, but realise he's showing me the time before my last birth when I chose my physical life and everyone and everything in it. Weirdly, the process is both longer and shorter than I imagined.

Even more extraordinary, I understand why the energetic figure that is me is so enthusiastic about wanting to experience a physical life filled with exceptional challenges. It's clear from my confidence that this isn't the first time I'm choosing such a life. The image that is me is animated, talking about how fantastic it would be to contribute something profound to everyone. Evidently, *that* me believe it's possible and is excited I'll have gone through a life no one would expect, and wants it to be inspiring.

Grand ambitions indeed. And how I've failed.

I'm looking at the image of myself in disbelief. What was I thinking? I wonder how I came up with such crazy ideas. But it seemed easy then – and now, for that matter – to imagine living a life of challenges. The others, sitting around me as they are now, agreed.

I'd sigh if I could. But either I'm unable to do so, or more likely, I can't scrape up the will to do so.

I look at the people around me.

What did they know about that life? Here, where we are now, where all is white and pure, it all seems so easy. No messy love stories or human misery and dramas live here.

I step away in near disgust and turn my back to the holographic image.

Perhaps I've been too recently in the physical world to appreciate the esoteric thoughts around loftier goals and intentions?

The others in the theatre are still in their seats. They're focussed on my reaction. I wait for their disapproval, but their eyes show only warmth and friendliness. There's no judgement in their eyes or energy, as though I didn't fail.

Have they seen my recent lifetime yet? Perhaps they were waiting for me to get here and watch the movie of my life, to witness my failure with me, so they can rub it in?

The thoughts of a small girl with golden curls near the middle of the group reach me. Her energy feels familiar, and in my mind, her voice is high, soft and clear, like a crystal wind chime.

"We are your soul tribe, Lee, so we experience everything with you. But you're right. We weren't all there with you. So, not all of us have experienced your life, nor have we seen the movie of your life yet. It's why we're here now – to help, as you've helped us in our chosen lives many times before."

I'm surprised to hear I've helped, but I'm unnerved as I realise they can hear my thoughts. James seemed to be able to do so and I thought it was only him that could hear them. I guess it makes a kind of sense as everything else in this place does.

I must be more careful.

No sooner do I think this than everyone laughs. The voices resonate through my mind and create a scintillating rainbow of sound.

James walks over and puts an arm around my shoulders.

"You can't hide your thoughts from us here, Lee. Just as we can't hide ours from you. But because you've been in a physical form recently, you're unused to who you really are. It won't take you long to adjust to this reality. Don't worry."

At once, I forget to be careful and can't stop my thoughts. "But how...?"

"Just as you're experiencing our energy and thoughts, we can hear yours, see them and feel your energy because we're all connected – we're all one."

I've heard something about everyone being one before, but dismissed it then as I do now. It can't be true. People are individuals, separate from each other. These people here are individuals, too, clearly. I can see them-each one sitting in their own chair.

Again, a ripple of laughter goes through the people surrounding the stage.

But James doesn't laugh. Instead, he squeezes my shoulders.

"We only appear to be separate, Lee. Anything that happens to one of us results in all of us experiencing it."

My expression of incredulity spurs James on to elaborate.

"We may not experience things directly, but the consciousness of which we're all a part learns and expands, which means we all learn and expand."

I must continue to look confused because James resumes.

"Do you remember when the teacher told your class about the hundredth monkey phenomenon in primary school? Apparently, monkeys who lived on an island had amazed the scientists when first one monkey, then the rest-about a hundred-started washing the mud from their food one day?"

I can feel myself nodding as James continues to send his thoughts to my mind.

"Do you remember the other team of scientists on another island reported that the monkeys there had started doing the same thing shortly afterwards? They'd been amazed because the monkeys from the islands had had no contact with one another?"

I understand what James is saying, but I'm still not convinced his example means we're all one.

Evidently, he sees my disbelief because he continues.

"I'm sure you know we're all the same energy, the same consciousness. The only reason we appear separate is that our frequencies are slightly different. The problem is we believe we're separate, finite beings, especially in our physical forms.

"Do you remember I told you we have amnesia in our physical forms? Apparently, we created beliefs to fill in our amnesia, and the most dangerous belief is that we're not one energy, one consciousness, but that we're separate from each other."

The thought escapes me before I can check it.

"Why is that a dangerous belief?"

This time, an older man with long white hair and a beard to match answers my thought question.

"Because when we believe we're separate, we can mistreat each other, be unkind, unjust, and in ways you wouldn't want anyone else to treat you. That's one reason the world is so full of struggle and sorrow."

I understand what he's saying, and I agree. But I wonder what the point is.

Again, I forget they can hear my thoughts, and the young girl responds again.

"Only by limiting itself in each of us can consciousness perceive and observe itself. It's the way it learns and expands. When you experience something, all of consciousness, all of us, expand because of your experience."

I turn to look at James.

"Okay, actually that makes sense. It's what you were talking about that night at my flat. But how did you know about it in your physical form?"

James's smile is radiant.

"I guess I remembered it. But also, it's why I used drugs. I felt strongly I was being held in bondage and wanted to break through what I perceived as reality. I felt drugs would allow me to enter an altered consciousness so I could see the truth that I suspected was hiding from me in my human form."

The man with the long white hair and beard adds to James's ideas.

"Sometimes, that fractured part of consciousness that focuses itself on seemingly individual parts of itself is more self-aware. In our physical form, we call those people psychics or sensitives. James was one of those."

I can feel myself nodding again.

"Yes, that's how I experienced James. He was a sensitive. It's what my mother used to call such people too. She said she was one, and so was I. It's why we were different from the rest of the family."

The young girl's thoughts reach me.

"I said that, dear Lee, because it was true."

I turn towards her.

"Wait. What? You mean you were my mother? But you're just a child."

Another collective ripple of laughter flows through my mind as the young girl responds.

"I was indeed the human you called Mother in your most recent life, Lee. But I'm here now in my entirety because I've already left the physical world, though I understand you haven't viewed that part of your life on the Earth plane yet."

I run towards her, falling at her feet and burying my head in her lap, my arms around her small waist.

"Oh, my God! Did I get to say goodbye to you, Mother? You must know, despite everything – your harshness, neglect and the hurt you've caused, I love you."

The young girl strokes my head, but another, deeper male voice to my right reaches my mind. I see a younger man with thick black hair who directs his thought voice to me.

"The aspect of the one consciousness you called Mother is an Ascended Master, Lee. She agreed to help create the challenges you wanted to experience out of love. Her appearance here as a child shows the extreme purity of her soul, of that fragment of consciousness she represents."

"Thank you. That actually makes sense. I didn't think anyone would deliberately be that cruel to their children. There had to be something behind it. I guess amnesia is part of this experience too, and not only on Earth."

James helps me up and leads me back to the stage.

"That's why we're showing you this now, Lee. This was when you chose your life and everything in it, and once you see it again, you'll remember everything."

I shake my head and look at the hologram with the fog swirling around inside it.

"I still disagree. No one would choose my life. You said it's because I wanted to expand and help everyone else and all consciousness expand. But surely there must be other, less horrible ways to do so?"

James and I lock eyes. I'm still surprised by how blue his eyes are here, though I'm unsure what I expected.

His gaze intensifies as he responds.

"It's odd that we learn more through pain and struggle in our human forms. But you're right, Lee. There are other, less horrible ways to expand and help others to do so too. Let's look at your pre-incarnation requests, shall we?"

James turns back to the hologram and swipes a hand over it.

At once, the fog clears, and I watch the image of myself excitedly talking about how I can make my life extraordinarily difficult. I witness my thoughts saying if I survived long enough to learn something profound, then all of consciousness would expand that much faster. Hence, we'd all get an upgrade, so to speak.

Oh, I see. So, I did believe in one consciousness before this incarnation.

Relief washes over me as I watch my soul group asking pertinent questions about several of my wilder ideas. It reigned me in a little. I'm grateful they were there because who knows what craziness I would have wanted without their wise counsel and guidance.

CHAPTER 13

I WATCH FOR MOMENTS, and I'm amazed that I chose everything I wanted in my physical life. I'm even more surprised about how I came to those choices. If I'd never seen this for myself, I would never have imagined it. Even while watching it all play out on the hologram before me, I still don't believe it.

James glances at me, a smile curling around his mouth.

"It's hard to believe, right? We feel things happen to us randomly in our physical bodies. It seems we have no control over whatever life throws at us. And it's a shock to realise we chose it all. But because it's a vibrational choice, things don't happen quite the way we might imagine. The fact remains, we choose the lessons, the learning opportunities."

Even my voice in my head is sounding different as I respond to him. Perhaps I'm reverting to who I am as he said I would? I'm not all that comfortable with it. I'm quite used to who I've been so far, thankyouverymuch.

"Yes, I understand it, though I still find the whole thing bizarre. I mean, we put ourselves through all this crap just so everyone can expand and learn? Learn what, though?"

Behind me, the young girl with the golden curls responds.

"Our learning leads to a deeper understanding, Lee. Not only of ourselves, but of life itself, of consciousness. The age-old questions of who and why we are, are still relevant. If we, as individuals, pose these questions, then all consciousness would want answers to those same questions, too, don't you think? Consciousness is all-pervasive. Without it, nothing exists, not even the smallest atom. I'm sure you've learned of the split atom experiment?"

I can feel myself nodding.

At last, someone is saying something I can remember and understand in a way that will hopefully make all this make sense.

Again, my thought voice sounds different from what I'm used to – somehow more musical. Do I imagine the change in resonance too?

"Yes, when the experiment was observed, it produced a different result than when it wasn't being observed."

The young girl's voice smiles in my head.

"Indeed. Since you're a fragment of consciousness, doesn't it tell you something about consciousness? I believe in the physical world, it's still referred to as the ocean in a drop."

I grasp what she says at once, and now I understand it. How did I never see it before?

I turn to face her.

"You mean whatever I put my conscious focus on changes its behaviour as I focus on it? Then how will I ever know its authentic behaviour without my focus on it?"

A many-voiced ripple of laughter flows through my mind, and I understand everyone is enjoying this conversation.

Once the multi-coloured sounds die down, the girl's voice glides through my mind, pure and comforting.

"You're absolutely right, Lee. It's almost impossible to see the true nature of anything because observing it changes its behaviour. It's because consciousness is everywhere in everything. In the physical world, it's even more difficult to understand, but even the air you breathed there, was consciousness."

I can feel myself nod again.

"I understand now, and I can see it. Nothing can exist without the consciousness that permeates it. Yes, it makes sense. But I still don't understand why horrible things would happen. Do you mean we choose those things too?"

This time, a beautiful woman with a mane of sparkling red hair responds, her voice rippling through my mind like the coolest water.

"I know it's difficult to believe when we see and hear of atrocities and how it seems to minimise the value of human life. But suppose you remember you are not who you think and instead know you are a mere fragment of the consciousness that brought this universe into being and many others, too. In that case, you'll understand that everything has value.

"Even when people go through the most horrific experiences imaginable, they have agreed to everything before that fragment of consciousness ever chose the life it wanted to experience.

"Consciousness is all there is.

"Becoming physical is the only way to observe itself and learn about itself, understanding its own wisdom, compassion, pain, and love.

"Life in our physical forms takes but a fraction of time, so it's so precious. You can't choose the same life again. Once you've lived a specific life, you may choose another. But you will have been changed by your previous experiences, and you will have evolved to choose a deeper, more profound experience next time.

"It's why you are consciousness's unique manifestation in every life you choose to live. It's also why, what you call terrible experiences in your physical form, are as valuable as wonderful experiences."

I pace as I think-speak.

"Right, so horrible things happen to good people because we choose it. That's what you're saying?"

James's voice slides through my mind as he walks with me.

"It's where our free will comes in, Lee. We choose it, yes, but we choose it through our frequency and not necessarily the actual event.

"If you remember you are but a fragment of the overall consciousness of everything, then it will make more sense to you. It means that things appear to be harmful to us in our physical forms, especially. But everything is allowed-the good, the bad, the ugly-for the experience, the learning, understanding and expansion of all consciousness. We can't learn anything without experiencing it.

"It's why you saw your non-physical fragment of consciousness being excited at the prospect of choosing a life filled with challenges. In your non-physical state, you understood this simple concept. You were enthusiastic about participating in the expansion, knowledge and growth we're all here for."

I stop pacing and face James.

"I understand what you're saying. But it's difficult to reconcile the evil, injustice and horror of physical life."

The young girl with the golden curls responds.

"That's why you're making these choices in your non-physical state, Lee. Here, the only emotion we experience is love."

I gaze at her, still amazed that this is the non-physical entity I called Mother.

"So, you're saying we choose everything from a place of love?"

Her smile lights up the space.

"Indeed."

As I contemplate this, I wonder if the overwhelming presence I feel around me is the love she mentioned. I've never experienced such peace in my life as I do here. It's why I'm finding watching episodes of my life more and more difficult because I don't want to be reminded of the emotions I felt in the moments I'm witnessing.

James responds quickly to my thoughts as though to soothe me.

"It's why we're showing you everything, Lee. So, now you know why you've chosen the life you did, it's time for you to watch more of it to understand the lessons you've learned from it."

I'd sigh if I could.

"Must I?"

The red-headed woman gets up and walks towards me.

"Just as the consciousness that is everything experiences physical life through every fragment that agrees to become focused on physicality, you must watch your life to understand your growth and expansion. If you choose another physical life, this understanding will be invaluable in choosing something that will take you deeper into a more profound understanding of consciousness and love."

A thought occurs to me.

"But if consciousness is forever expanding and growing through every fragmented part of itself that materialises, do we ever catch up and get to know it? Is there ever an end to what consciousness can learn? When will it know itself?"

The other members of my soul tribe get up and form a smaller circle around me on the stage.

The older man with the white hair and beard smiles as he nods.

"Ah, that's the question, isn't it? Haven't you noticed you learn something about yourself in every new incident that you could not have known without the experience? Once you've learned, understood and come to know something through experience, you can never not know it. If it's true for each of us, how much more true must it be for all of consciousness?"

I wonder if my soul tribe can see my thoughts as an image of the ever-expanding universe in which we live our physical lives appears in my mind's eye, and beyond it, the Glome.

CHAPTER 14

I RESENT NED SPRAWLING all over my bed like he owns both our beds. I mean, why can't he sit on his own? But I reckon he'd throw a proper tantrum if I sat on his, though, won't he?

Focussing my anger on Ned as hard as I can, I try to imitate the angry expression on Ned's face. It's the only way I can get the Glome under control. But I don't know how long I can keep it up.

It's true, though. If anyone should be hopping crazy mad, it should be me. How could I have been so bloody stupid to believe Ned? Again. And go along with his ridiculous, stupid bloody plans. Again. What the hell is the matter with me? I mean, rob a bank? Who does that any more? It wasn't snatching nibbles from a corner shop like we did at school. Robbing a bank is on a whole other level.

I knew I should have refused when Ned brought the gun to my house. But I didn't want a fuss, and I was too shocked at his audacity. I had to get him out of there quickly. After hiding the gun under my bed, I took him round the corner to the pub. I had to get him away from Grandmother and Mother.

I should have known then it would all end badly. But prison. Shit, man. It's not funny. Grandmother is going to kill me. I'm supposed to put the bins out tonight.

Why couldn't I just tell Ned to shove the bloody gun where the sun doesn't shine?

Apparently, I'm as gutless as the Glome is fierce. But since it perceives I'm angry this time, it's watching to see what I'll do, how I'll exact my revenge on Ned. I can feel it observing me, waiting.

It's not an act on my part. I can't fool the Glome, anyway. I'm genuinely as pissed off as I've ever been. But truthfully, I'm angrier at myself than Ned. Why do I always get myself into these bloody situations with him?

I can't control my anger and slam my fist into the wall beside me. But instead of lessening my feelings, I feel fire building in my chest.

Ned is still sitting on my bed. But now, the frown of thunder on his face has been replaced by that ridiculous smirk he wears when he thinks he's sooo superior to everyone else.

His voice is acidic and mocking.

"Careful, little one. You'll hurt your soft, artsy hands."

He speaks as he gets up. As always, his smirk is the predecessor to the violence he habitually inflicts on those who dare to offend him.

He stops inches from my face and points his finger almost up inside my nostril.

"You better start praying they don't keep me in here with you, Lee. You had one job to do. One!"

Ned's face turns puce as he jabs his finger on the scar across my left cheek.

"One.fuckin.job. And.you.couldn't.even.do.that."

I'd take a step backwards to get away from his finger and garlic breath, but I'm already against the wall.

I can feel the Glome moving inside me, reaching to connect with the fire that blazed briefly in my chest but disappeared at Ned's approach. It's just as well because I don't think I can deal with my own anger on top of battling the Glome and handling Ned as well.

Perhaps the Glome peeped out at Ned because his face suddenly turns white, and he backs away from me. Even his voice is weaker as he continues his threat.

"I'm just saying, Lee. You'd better pray I don't go down with you."

Ned's still walking backwards, all fire gone from him when a prison officer opens the door and interrupts Ned's words.

The sudden intrusion breaks the tension between Ned and me, though I understand the Glome's warning has impacted Ned's confidence.

The officer growls without looking at either of us.

"You two. Follow me."

I let Ned go first and follow behind as the guard leads us to the showers. I can smell the water and soap before we get there. My heart is beating in my neck, and my knees feel weak at having to shower with other prisoners because I've heard stories of the violence in the showers. But when we turn the corner, I almost sag with relief when I see no one else there.

The officer motions for us to enter.

"You have five minutes. Don't let me come in there."

He doesn't follow us inside, but shoves towels and clean orange overalls at us and waits outside.

Ned walks over to a bench and starts undressing, and I quickly follow his example, pulling off my shoes and throwing my clothes on the bench. The tiles are freezing under my feet, but I'm afraid of slipping, so I carefully make my way to the nearest shower.

There's no privacy, as the showers are all in one row against the wall. I don't have any soap or shampoo with me, but at least I'll be cleaner than I am now. There's nothing I can do about my clothes. When the police tackled me, I'd slipped on the rain-soaked lawn and not only was I drenched, but caked in mud too when they brought me in. Ned and the others didn't fare any better.

I'm guessing because they allow only two people per cell, Dave and Mick must be together in another.

The water isn't exactly hot, but at least the pressure is enough to wash away the mud from my hair, face and hands. The muddy water stings my eyes.

I feel, rather than see, Ned approaching me, and I know what he's going to do.

So, this is his revenge.

I brace myself.

His hand grabs my hair while with the other, he pushes me hard so I'm bent over. He's much stronger than I imagined, but I don't fight back. Even the Glome is silent, waiting, watching.

Then, pain. Searing pain.

But I take it. I don't cry out. I don't want the guard to witness my humiliation.

The water drowns out most of Ned's grunting noises as he violates me. His thrusts are filled with rage. I start to feel numb.

The smells and pain recede, and weirdly, I find comfort in being this close to Ned. I don't think we've ever even hugged, but I've always liked it when he put an arm around my shoulders. At the thought of feeling him like this, I feel myself responding and growing harder.

He grabs me tighter as he climaxes, and I can hear him struggling to stay silent. After moments, he pushes me from him and goes to clean himself a few showers away, ignoring me, his face red and glum.

For moments, my body stays in the position Ned pushed me. I'm too stunned to react or straighten. That he'd been so gentle with me at the end brings tears to my eyes. Perhaps it wasn't all rage and anger. Maybe he feels some kindness towards me, after all.

I can sense the Glome staring at Ned, but he doesn't come out, and I'm aware of its confusion as much as my own.

CHAPTER 15

W E FOLLOW THE OFFICER back to our cell in silence, not making eye contact.

I try not to show through my gait what just happened to me, but I can't unfeel Ned on my body, Ned inside me.

The officer unlocks our cell and waits for us to enter before he locks it behind us again.

I walk to my bed and just as I mean to sit down, my legs give way. The enormity of what happened between Ned and me hits me at that moment. I fall down on my bed and don't hide my feelings of confusion and anger from Ned.

I feel his eyes on me. But I'm still dealing with the Glome. Its energy is turbulent, seething, but unlike me, it doesn't appear as astonished as I am. How could this be my reality right now?

The Glome wants to look at Ned, but I refuse. Instead, I want to escape Ned, but the cell is small, and there's no hiding from him. I feel Ned continuing to stare at me, and when I look up, his face carries a weird look I don't like.

I decide to take the defensive route with him.

"What you staring at?"

I try to sound angry, but even I can hear the quiver of fear in my voice.

What makes the situation even more stressful for me is Ned's silence. He says nothing, just stares at me with that odd expression on his face. It's as though he's seeing me for the first time, but he's also looking at me as though I'm his favourite dessert.

What to make of it?

Sod it. Let him be weird. I don't care.

I turn my head away, cross my ankles and put my arms behind my head, staring up at the ceiling. It's grey and dull. I focus on a small black spot. It's not much, but anything is better than looking at Ned's strange eyes.

The Glome has calmed somewhat inside me, but I feel the darkness that personifies him waiting, and I don't like it. There's anticipation in the Glome's silence.

It seems like forever before Ned speaks.

"I'm sorry, okay?"

His voice is soft, and he sounds remorseful.

But I've known him since our high school days, and I had trouble trusting anything he said then. Now, he's landed us in gaol, for heaven's sake, and especially after what just happened in the showers, there's no way I'll believe him again.

I don't look at him. I keep staring at the ceiling.

He continues to speak to me, his voice becoming more assertive and louder as he continues.

"Did you hear me? I said I'm sorry."

I still don't look at him, and I don't respond.

Ned is shifting around on his bed, and I imagine him sitting up against the wall, his arms crossed over his muscled chest.

His voice continues to drip confidence in that well-known way. I know it's his attempt to be persuasive. It's always made me believe he'd make a great salesman.

"Come on. Don't tell me you didn't enjoy it. You wanted it as much as I did. But you took me by surprise. I never realised this is what you wanted from me. I always thought you were more interested in girls."

What?

I can't even get my head around Ned's words. He's got the audacity to blame me for what he just did to me.

I say nothing. What's the point?

By Ned's movements, it's obvious he's getting more pissed off. I don't know what he's doing, but I can hear him shuffling and scuffling.

Suddenly, he's above me, grabbing my arms, holding them down, his knees on my thighs.

At first, I'm shocked. I try to push him away from me, but then I think, what's the point? If he could do what he did in the shower with the guard just outside the door, what prevents him from doing whatever he wants when there's no one here to see him?

I'm staring at Ned now, unable to look away from his face. It's brimming with anger and something else. If I were a betting man, I'd say it's lust. But surely not...

He licks his lips as though he's going to enjoy a tasty meal, his eyes remaining on my mouth.

Please don't kiss me. Please don't kiss me.

I roll my lips together so tight, I'm sure they don't even look like lips anymore.

Ned's Adam's Apple moves up and down on his tanned neck as he swallows hard.

His voice sounds strange, husky when he speaks.

"You made me do it, Lee. I've never done it before, and if not for you, I'd never have done it. I swear."

He lets go of my arms and shoves a hand across my mouth. His eyes have changed. The colour has almost completely disappeared in the black of his dilated pupils.

"Don't speak. Don't say anything. I want to look at you this time."

As Ned speaks, he wriggles out of his pants and undoes mine, and all I can think is, "No, not again. Stop."

But Ned's hands on my shoulders are strong. He's pinned me to the bed with his knees. He spreads my legs, trying to gain entrance. To my utter consternation, I feel myself respond when his hand brushes over me and I feel him pushing against me.

Then everything happens so fast. It's like lightning, and I feel like I'm dreaming for a second.

Ned is bleeding, holding his neck, and I'm torn between fury about Ned's actions, and accepting this is perhaps the only way Ned can love me.

Until now, I hadn't realised I had always yearned for Ned's love. Perhaps it's why I've always gone along with his dodgy schemes. The undeniable truth that I'd longed for his love, even if it looks like this, almost knocks me sideways.

But fury wins.

I feel my energy extending as the Glome stops my body from moving. It's as though something rips my chest apart from the inside out. It's excruciating, and I almost cry out, biting my lips shut instead. I force myself to be still and silent. My eyes are closed tight, and I feel tears squeezing out the corners, but I hear the sickening thud of Ned's head hitting the wall opposite my bed.

Ned's making strangled, gurgling noises, and it's clear he's in serious trouble. But the Glome hasn't finished. His presence pervades the small cell, and his smell is everywhere, musky and intense. His enormity has snuffed out the light behind my closed eyelids. I see only blackness.

I don't know if I've manifested the Glome or if he's here of his own accord, but I know he's enormous, dark-black, and he's in full revenge mode on Ned. But somehow, the noises fade into the background as I focus on breathing. I'm not scared, but I don't want to open my eyes, don't want to be a witness to the Glome's ferocious presence. I'd rather not see what he's doing to Ned.

I T SEEMS AGES HAD passed as I lay there, eyes closed against the darkness that wouldn't leave, listening to the sounds of the Glome punishing Ned, whose groans become weaker and weaker. Ned is silent, and I know he's dead.

I wait.

Behind my eyelids, I still see only darkness in the cell, but feel the Glome's enormity and all-pervasiveness. I'm aware the Glome is gathering itself, preparing to re-enter me.

I brace myself for the pain I know will assault my body and senses and pinch every muscle in my face. Each nail digs into my palms as I resolve to make no noise during the process.

Let it be quick.

———— *ele* ————

I MUST HAVE FALLEN asleep or passed out, or something because I awake to a prison officer's rough hands grabbing me and cuffing me.

There are no lights in the cell, but light streams through the open door. I see Ned's mangled corpse lying opposite my bed against the wall, bloodied and unrecognisable. Dark red splashes of his blood against the wall reach the ceiling.

The officer pulls me up, but my trousers have pooled around my ankles, and I stumble as I try to walk ahead of the shove he gives my back. Another joins us, I'm guessing, to make sure I don't attack and kill one of their colleagues.

As I walk along the corridor, I hear the officers whispering behind me.

"In all my years here, I've seen nothing like it."

And the other voice filled with awe.

"Yeah. Going down for murder for sure."

My new cell is tiny, very dark, very silent.

I'm alone. Solitary confinement.

In the overwhelming silence, I still see the guards looking at each other, then at me, fear and confusion clear in their eyes.

Ned's crushed corpse lies in a large, dark pool. Not a drop of blood is on me.

CHAPTER 16

THE GLOME LIKES SOLITARY confinement even less than I do.

Whenever the guard comes to deliver my food and meds, the Glome tries to engage him in conversation.

When the officer leaves, the Glome and I always argue. Often our screaming matches are so loud it hurts my ears, and I'm afraid the prison officers will hear us and punish me even more.

But the Glome doesn't care, and sometimes our arguments last hours. Mainly, we argue about Ned and getting out of here. I'm not sure why we're fighting. We both want the same thing.

But the officers never respond to the Glome, only pushing the food through the hole in the wall.

I hear the guard at the wall and sigh as I go to retrieve the plastic bowl from the shelf where it's been shoved. You can't call it food. I'm not sure what it is, but the consistency is like porridge and smells disgusting. Larger, more solid pieces suggest meat has been added, but I can't taste what it is, so it's probably chicken.

The broth is lukewarm and horrible, but I gulp it down because it makes me feel a little warmer and takes away the pain in my stomach. I know this feeling far too well.

I'm transported back to my childhood, sharing the flat in Ireland with Mother, Mary and Connor and later with Grandmother when she joined us.

In my mind's eye, I see Mother lying on the red sofa and almost jump out of my skin when the door suddenly opens.

An officer stands in the light streaming in from outside. He's still, and I have a bad feeling about his unusual behaviour.

Even his voice is softer and seems gentler. But perhaps I'm just unused to hearing someone talking to me.

"Get up. Face the wall."

I follow his instructions and face the wall beside my bed, my hands on the wall above my head.

I'm used to this procedure. It happens every day when I'm taken to the shower. Thankfully, I'm always alone in the shower now. Not even the officer follows me in there.

But I'm sure it's not time for my shower yet, and something feels different this time.

I sense the officer continuing to stand in the doorway. For a moment, I wonder if I'm being moved to another cell.

His steps are quick as he walks forward and cuffs me.

I move to turn around, but his words slap me.

"Stay where you are! Face the wall!"

After a moment of silence in which I'm acutely aware of his nearness, he speaks again, his voice softer, like before.

"There's news from your family. Your mother has died."

I'm frozen. I don't know what to feel. But my body knows and responds. My heart pounds in my chest. My mouth opens as my breathing increases. Tears drip down my chin.

I want to ask, "how?" But I know there won't be an answer. Another set of footsteps enters my cell. Another voice barks.

"Turn around."

I do as I'm told.

An older, much larger officer stands near the door, his hand on a pistol holder at his side. He cocks his head.

"Walk."

I'm aware the other officer is behind me, following into the bright lights of the corridor that always hurts my eyes, and I blink away more tears.

I stop at the door that divides the prison into sections. The officer who'd cuffed me unlocks the door with a deadening clunking sound that reverberates throughout the building.

For moments, I'm mesmerised, as always, by the enormous bunch of keys in his hands. How on earth does he remember which key is for what door? I've never had a key before. Not when we lived in Ireland and not at the house here in Liverpool.

Someone always let me in. Now, there was only Grandmother.

Fresh tears run down my cheeks at the thought, but I make no sound, biting my lips together instead.

I don't know why I'm sad. My relationship with Mother wasn't good. But I saw the beauty of her soul buried deep inside her and her struggle to keep it hidden. I always wondered why she did that.

I walk unseeing behind the officer in an unfamiliar part of the prison until we reach a door with a blue plaque on it. Bold gold letters read, "Prison Warden."

The officer knocks, and after hearing a voice calling, "Come," he opens the door, standing aside for me to enter.

A man with neat grey hair and kind ocean-coloured eyes looks up over glasses balancing on his nose.

He nods and gestures for me to sit in front of his desk.

I feel the two officers who'd accompanied me, standing directly behind me.

Guess I'm still regarded as a dangerous criminal.

The Warden removes his glasses and takes me in with those blue eyes before he speaks.

"We're all sorry for your loss, Lee. It's been brought to my attention that you've been an exemplary inmate here."

I sit still. Inside me, the Glome is as still, waiting.

"Because of it and your young age, you'll be transferred to a regular cell. If all goes well, you may be granted special permission to attend your mother's funeral, accompanied by two officers. Understand I said, 'may.' If anything... anything happens, that causes me to withdraw this offer, you will be detained in solitary confinement again."

Though his words are harsh, his voice is soft and kind.

"Do you understand?"

I nod, but the Glome uses my voice.

"Yes, I do. Thank you. It would mean everything to attend my mother's funeral and to see my grandmother and siblings. I'm very grateful and will do everything in my power not to disappoint you. I promise."

Even I'm astonished at the Glome's eloquence and the surprising way he uses my voice so melodiously. It's almost entrancing, and the effect on the Warden is immediate.

I notice his eyes glaze over as though he's been drugged, and I wonder if the Glome has had a similar effect on the officers behind me. But I don't turn around. I stay still.

After moments, the Warden seems to snap out of his stupor. He cleans his glasses with the bottom of his tie, and before he places them back on his nose, I notice the little groove they've carved where they habitually sit.

He stares at me for a long time.

"Good. I'm glad we understand each other, Lee."

Then he breaks eye contact and appears to busy himself with the work on his desk.

I've been dismissed.

But the Glome has other ideas. He clears my throat.

"May I ask, will I be alone in the cell? It's just... Coming out of solitary into contact with so many other people may... overstimulate me?"

I'm shocked but stay as still as the Glome, my eyes never leaving the Warden's face.

Has the Glome overstepped the mark?

The Warden's face is unreadable when he looks up. He nods slightly and waves with the back of his hand.

It must be something the officers behind me understand because they grip my shoulders and pull me out of the chair, marching me through the door and back along the corridor again. As we walk, I become aware of other prisoners, their voices, their smell, their heaviness. It's as though I'm walking through a thick veil of noise and human thoughts.

My pulse is beating in my neck, and I almost collapse in gratitude when the officers unlock a cell door, indicating for me to enter. The unused beds and toilet show I'll be alone in this cell, and I'm immediately grateful.

I do as I'm told, turn around and feel the cuffs removed from my wrists. I stay facing the wall until I hear the door bang shut behind me, the key turning in the lock.

There are others around me. I bask in their nearness, their presence, but I'm grateful I don't have to be too close to any of them.

The Glome and I are both silent in our cell, listening to the sounds surrounding us. We make out snippets of conversations, but nothing too precise. It's weirdly comforting. I lie down on the narrow, hard bed and interlace my fingers behind my head.

WHEN THE GUARD POKES my foot with his baton, the first thing on my mind is, "It's today."

As the days went by, the surrounding noise intensified. Probably because my hearing became clearer as I entered the world again. It's one reason I've been looking forward to this day and escaping the constant noise around me, even if only for a few hours.

I sit up and nod at the officer standing outside my cell door. The dark suit, white shirt and black tie lay at the foot of my bed where the guard had placed it the night before. I'm grateful Grandmother sent Conor to the prison with the clothes. It would have been too humiliating to attend my mother's funeral in my prison uniform.

Throwing the blanket from my body, I get up, brush my teeth, wash my face and get dressed as quickly as possible, aware of the officer's presence outside my door. Even though he's standing with his back towards me, I'm shy and eager to hide my nakedness from him. But it's not possible in this kind of open cell, so I dress as fast as I can, sitting on the bed to hide as I put on the shirt, then the pants first. Socks, shoes, tie and jacket are last. The suit feels heavy and suffocating, and I'm not sure I got my tie straight. Running my fingers along the buttoned-up collar of my shirt, I try to create a little more space to breathe easier. I push my hands through my hair, turn to the wall, and put both hands above my head.

My voice doesn't sound like mine when I speak.

"Ready."

I hear the guard unlocking my door. His footsteps are quick and impatient as he walks to cuff my hands and yanks me towards the door ahead of him.

In the corridor, we're joined by another officer who walks ahead of me and unlocks the doors as we meet them.

My heart pulses in my neck, and I feel energy surge through my body as we near the door to the outside world.

I can't help but stop for a moment as I step outside the prison. The sun burns bright through the suit, and I lift my face and close my eyes, aware that my nostrils have flared as I inhale deep lungfuls of air I recognise at once. It has notes of freedom, the smell of fuel and the heat of the sun and the earth. I didn't know I'd missed it so much.

But the officers hurry me to a waiting police van and shove me inside. I almost press my face against the window to take in as much of the world as possible. I want the journey to be longer, but we reach the cemetery sooner than expected.

People are standing in small groups, all dressed in black, looking sombre. Mary's beautiful dark hair and Grandmother's short, grey curls are what I recognise first.

I'm suddenly nervous about how I'll be received. Perhaps I should leave. But my family has seen me, and there's no escape. I suppose the police van is a giveaway.

As they approach the van, I notice Conor has joined them. They look so stiff and smart and like strangers in their formal clothes. Conor carries the energy of the successful businessman he has become. Mary has turned into a young lady overnight, and Grandmother seems ancient, her back bent against life's onslaught and losing both her children.

I want to feel sorry for her, glad to see them, sad that Mother has died... something. But I feel nothing.

The officers help me from the van.

Mary approaches me first, hesitation clear in her manner and eyes. Her voice sounds strained and tight.

"Good to see you, Lee."

Her eyes flick from one guard to the next as she speaks fast.

"How are you? I've tried to visit, but you were in solitary."

A tiny, sad smile touches her lips.

"No visitors allowed. Glad you could come today."

I'm sure she wants to hug me but stops herself and takes a step back instead.

Just as Grandmother and Conor nod at me, the hearse carrying Mother's coffin arrives.

CHAPTER 17

THE YOUNG GIRL WITH the golden curls comes to stand beside me. I'm aware of her warmth and hand in mine as though we both have substance here.

Her thoughts caress my mind, even though I can't look at her.

"I know those who stay behind miss us when we leave our earthly lives. Even though our life together was challenging, your sadness at my passing soothed me. It made me feel I was important to you then. I know now, in the non-physical, we had agreed to everything important to us both before that life."

To us both?

I turn to her.

"You mean I was also important there for you?"

Sounds of her delighted laughter fill my mind.

"Oh, yes, my darling. We're all constantly evolving, even if in service to one another. Sharing that life with you taught me much and assisted my expansion, for which I'm grateful."

A thought enters my mind, and before I can conceal it, I feel the minds around me, leaning in like a hug.

"You've mentioned the only emotion we experience here is love. Is that the permeating force I've felt since I died in my physical life?"

"Yes, indeed. Love is Consciousness and the only reality. We know you can't see it yet, Lee. But it's everything. Nothing can exist without it, not us, not you. Consciousness is Love, and Love is Consciousness."

I'm relieved my mind is still intact, thinking the immense energy I've been aware of since my death was anything remotely like the Glome.

As though the souls around me understand my sudden epiphany, their silence envelops me. Their subtle and gentle urging gives me the confidence to open myself up to the massive Love energy surrounding me.

I spread my arms. I'm ready.

At first, the light around me increases though I didn't think it was possible. It should hurt. I'm sure I wouldn't have been able to bear it in my physical life. But here, the intensity changes from yellow to white to undulating rainbows of colours I've never seen, never knew existed. I see inside my companions, my soul tribe, who they really are, their beauty, compassion, and love. It's overwhelming but fantastically so.

The lights and colours of the incredible Love energy permeate my body in a soothing, gentle way, as though asking permission first, even though I'm aware none is required. I feel I'm being downloaded with the full, deep knowledge and understanding that the Love and Consciousness are the same. It creates everything, including me.

One moment, I understand it, feel comfortable and comforted, and then the knowledge, the feeling, seems to retreat from me. Like the whisps of a dream, it's just out of reach. At once, I crave its assurance, warmth and certainty. If I could still breathe, I'd be hyperventilating now.

But fear will not rule me. I fight the paralysing panic rising in me, determined to stay open to the Love. Deep knowledge inside me confirms it's pivotal to the next phase of whoever I am, whatever I'm becoming, and I will never be the same after this.

Brief thoughts of the Glome enter my mind, and again, I fight the dread of losing him and having to fight him anew.

But the Love, the warmth of it, mercifully continues to pervade my being, pouring peace into me like a shower of joy that touches every fibre in my being, assuring safety.

I realise my temporary panic was entirely self-induced. If I relax and allow myself to be open to the Love, I can experience it as fully as I dare. But my psyche is still attached to my earthly life, and shades of abandonment and rejection surface to constrict me.

But the Love appears to understand me entirely. Again, it envelops me gently before I perceive its power flowing through me. I calm down.

The Love's flow creates a feeling of floating. Looking down at myself, I see I'm no longer standing on the stage but hovering slightly above it, as are the others surrounding me.

I feel broken open, love pouring out of me, through me, merging with the Love I can now fully experience. There is nothing but the Love, and the deep peace that moves through me feels like I'm finally home.

I'm aware of the others as denser fragments of the Love, and for the first time, I understand completely that we are indeed all one, one Love. Nothing else exists. It is the most creative, harmonious Power in existence, and I'm a tiny, perfect out-picturing of it. Like the others, I experienced emotions, events and circumstances in a much denser physical reality through which we all expand as one Consciousness. It finally makes sense.

But suppose I was still in my physical body. In that case, I'm sure I would have been crying at the beauty of it all and the indescribable feelings of bliss and joy pouring through my heart as though it had burst apart.

I can still sense the subtle differences in energy representing the surrounding individuals, and I'm aware of James moving next to me. But he's not the James I once knew. His a far brighter energy.

His voice in my head has changed. The sound is clearer, deeper, and more melodious than before, and his voice was already incredible.

"There's nothing to be afraid of, Lee. You're in your most perfect expression of who you are now."

I feel it. I understand. But as though my mind was locked up in my physical life, and is now free of all constraints, all boundedness, I'm brimming with questions. The first rises to the surface.

How are we individualised if we're One Love, One Consciousness?

James's energy flares for a moment as though his thoughts affect his being.

"We aren't really individualised. We only think we are and in our physical forms, it's much easier to think of ourselves as individuals. But at our deepest spiritual core, we remain One Love, One Consciousness."

My thoughts turn again to the darkness that lived inside me. The Glome didn't feel like Love to me. How could it be part of the Consciousness when nothing can exist outside of the Consciousness and Love?

CHAPTER 18

IT ALL HAPPENED SO fast.

One moment I was at Mother's funeral. The next, back in prison, sitting in front of the Warden.

And now, here I am, on a train heading to London.

My head is spinning.

There are no guards here.

After all that time, I'm free.

Getting my head around being in prison for three years is hard.

But where are my feelings? Had I left them behind in prison? I should be sad, angry... something. But I feel nothing. Well, not entirely nothing. I feel numb.

It's understandable why Grandmother has arranged for me to move to London. Liverpool, getting mixed up with Ned's gang and imprisonment, is trouble on a whole other level. Not something Grandmother wants to deal with, and who can blame her? My mother's death, Conor's leaving, and Mary's moving away have all taken their toll on Grandmother. The tiny flat the Council had offered her after Mother's death is too small for me to share, anyway.

But what awaits me in London? I suppose meeting a Grand-father I had never known before could be exciting. No one knows me there.

"A fresh start," Grandmother had said as she kissed my cheek and shoved a battered brown suitcase in my hand.

I don't suppose I'll ever see Grandmother again. Or Mary. Or Conor.

I sigh and lean back against the seat.

There aren't many people on the train, and I'm happy about it. I'm sleepy but fight to keep my eyes open, watching people get on and off the train through droopy lids. I don't want to miss anything. The green of the fields, the cheerful yellow of the oilseed rape and the darker green of the trees near the tracks whizz by, and I feel I could travel forever. I wish I could.

But as we get nearer to London, more buildings appear. Until the train pulls into the station, there are cute little villages and built-up areas.

Kings Cross is overwhelming. I stand, collect my suitcase and rucksack from the overhead rack, and follow several other passengers through the doors. At once, I'm swept along by the maelstrom of bodies making for the exit. It's suffocating. But I allow myself to be pushed through the turnstiles, across the concourse, and into the busy street.

Everything feels so different from Liverpool or Ireland. The buildings are beautiful as I thought London's buildings would be, and the people appear confident in their rush to get wher-ever they're going. I feel like an alien.

I pull the crumpled paper from my back pocket and reread the address. The taxi rank is easily recognisable, and I make my way there. I give the driver the paper with the address and get into the taxi. The driver is friendly and starts a conversation. I prefer to watch the people. Cars buzz along, and bikes dangerously escape collisions. We pass impressive buildings and massive parks as we make our way to my grandfather's house. It seems an eternity away from Central London.

Grandfather's house sits away from the quiet road, almost entirely obscured by massive trees. It must once have been a grand house, but now it's neglected, sad and old, just as I imagine Grandfather would look.

I pay the driver with the money Grandmother had given me. Holding my suitcase close to my body and my rucksack over my shoulder, I plod up the path with patches of broken slabs visible through the grass. The house looks more dilapidated as I get closer. With its peeling red paint, the front door reminds me briefly of the place in Liverpool when we'd first arrived from Ireland. But Grandfather's house, I know, will never be brought back to life again, as we did with our Liverpool home. But in its own way, Grandfather's house carries its fading beauty with dignity, and I can appreciate it.

I press the bell and hear it ringing somewhere in the depths of the house. Silence. Then heavy, slow footsteps approach the door from the inside. It creaks open a fraction in protest, as though not used to such brutality inflicted on it. From the gloom, a bald head with wispy white hair on the sides and a many-lined, surly face appears. Watery blue eyes peer at me.

We stare at each other for moments before I realise he's waiting for me to speak.

"Hi, Grandpa."

The watery eyes narrow for moments. A grunt precedes a voice as scraggly as his face.

"Best come in then."

The door protests more as the gap grows marginally larger, allowing me to squeeze in sideways.

The smell immediately transports me back to my first encounter with the Liverpool house again.

Continuing to walk like a crab, I follow my grandfather's bony, bent figure down the dim, narrow hallway, made narrower by the newspapers stacked on both walls. They tower above my head. If I hadn't been in solitary, I might have felt claustrophobic. What would happen if the stacks fell on me? Imagine that? Buried under a sea of old, yellowing newspapers.

The house feels dry and papery. A chalky taste sits in my throat, and I hope a glass of water will rescue me.

We continue to shuffle down a hallway that seems never-ending. But I spot a light ahead, and relief washes over me. The gloom was getting to me. I need to get out, breathe.

The end of the hallway is sudden. Three large windows on each side of the kitchen pour welcome light into the room. But nothing seems to have been cleaned for years. Most cupboards have no doors, and the linoleum is broken. Old, rusty engine parts stand dotted among dirty, chipped plates and mugs on the countertops. At least the table had old, yellowing newspapers, presumably to protect it from all the debris. It's impossible to imagine Grandmother living in such squalor. Maybe that's why they'd separated all those years ago.

My attention is on the sink, dripping tap and trying to spot a clean cup. I'm desperate to get the taste of dry decay out of my throat.

But Grandfather doesn't stop. He makes his way to the backdoor and turns the key, opening it.

"Come. Best get you to your room."

How odd. Why would my room be outside?

I don't question him. Follow him out of the house and draw deep breaths of early autumn air laden with the welcome scent of plants and trees covering the back garden. It's an untamed jungle, and I love it at once.

Grandfather leads me down a barely visible path towards a shed surrounded by trees. He pulls open the door that protests as much as the house's front door did and stands aside, gesturing for me to enter first.

I almost stumble over the rusty garden tools lying higgledy-piggledy on the floor. At the rear of the shed, I spot a rickety-looking camping bed. Thrown across is a thin, frayed mattress, a pillow in even worse condition, and a pink blanket that had seen better days. Nothing is clean or homely. Spider webs cover the ceiling and hang in the corners like bunched-up lace, revealed as the sun hits them through the dusty windows.

I turn back to see if Grandfather is joking. This couldn't be my room. Nobody would be expected to sleep here.

But Grandfather is already shuffling back to the house.

He lifts a hand as he goes, and his voice disappears with his retreating, so I only just make out his words.

"Make yourself comfy. You can use the kitchen and bathroom downstairs."

I look at the mix of coloured leaves on the ground beneath my feet. Then up at the ominous, cloudy sky. The wind growls through the shed louder than my stomach. One windowpane has a crack.

Oh, joy.

CHAPTER 19

I BARELY SLEPT FOR more than a few hours. Even my cell in prison wasn't this uncomfortable. The bed sags, and the mattress is so thin, I may as well have been sleeping on the floor. The wind howled through the shed all night leaving me shivering despite wearing almost all of my clothes.

I'm calculating my money in my head for the umpteenth time, wondering if I can afford to buy a good sleeping bag. I'll check in the house for a better, thicker mattress. There must be one and there has to be a way to make the shed more wind-proof and comfortable.

A sudden thought occurs. I check my phone.

Ah, the prison services person will visit me today and according to my calendar, they'll be here at noon. Would that give me enough time to do all the things I've planned?

I stare at the clock on my phone. It's six, too early to get up, but I do so anyway.

I attempt to stretch the aches out of my back and neck, and hear cracks and pops as I do so. Surely, at twenty-four, I'm too young for my body to sound this worn out? I know

I'm overweight but that's another matter and something I can rectify, I hope. Food has always been an issue with me and after therapy in prison, I understand it stems from my childhood when too much hunger ruled our home. It seems I'm still making up for that now.

The door creaks as I open the shed. Leaves crackle underfoot as I make my way towards the kitchen and I hope Grandfather has remembered to leave it unlocked for me. I have to use the bathroom rather urgently and could do with something hot to drink. I don't expect there'd be much to eat.

Turning the handle, to my relief, the door opens. I enter the bright, though dirty kitchen. It takes a few wrong doors before I find the bathroom. When I return to the kitchen, I'm surprised to find Grandfather there, making coffee.

His watery blue eyes turn on me and he lifts a chin in greeting. His bony hand pushes a mug of steaming coffee towards me on the table. There are no chairs, so I take the coffee and lean my sore back against one of the cupboards.

I like lots of sugar in my coffee but I can't see any and Grandfather offers none. Nevermind, I tell myself, the hot coffee is very welcome. I sip it so I don't burn my mouth, and I'm pleasantly surprised that it's excellent. Either that, or I'd become too used to the prison's shitty excuse for coffee.

I decide to tackle the most urgent task first.

"Grandpa, is there a better mattress for the bed in the shed? I hardly slept at all."

Again, Grandfather's eyes shift to me. He looks as though he's seeing me for the first time.

"Check upstairs. But leave my bedroom alone."

I want to ask which one is his, but he's already shuffling out of the kitchen. Following him, we make our way down the hall towards the stairs I passed yesterday. I'm still wary of the mountains of newspapers on either side of me. But now I can appreciate their weird, ordered elegance.

Grandfather goes up one step at a time and his wheezing starts to worry me the further we go into what seems an endless abyss of darkness.

I'm puffing as much as Grandfather by the time we reach the landing at the top. We're both holding on to the dusty, wooden bannister. After several minutes, Grandfather hobbles off through one of the doors and I hear his bed creak beneath his weight as he lies down. At least now I know which bedroom is his.

Several musty bedrooms and lots of coughing later, I find what I'm looking for. Under piles of old clothes, books and yet more yellowing, but thankfully, dry newspapers, I see a mattress similar in size to the camping bed in the shed.

I look around the room. It's smaller than the others. A child's room, perhaps?

I wonder whose it was? My mother's? I don't remember my mother ever coming to England. As far as I know, she'd always lived in Ireland.

I freeze. Something tugs at the back of my mind.

There was a man. An uncle. Her brother?

Something happened. Something bad. Something involving the Glome.

I shake my head.

I don't want to think about the Glome now. He's been quiet since our conversation with the Warden had resulted in our freedom. I'm aware of him, of course, but grateful he's been behaving himself.

I remove everything from the bed. But there's nowhere to put the stuff, so I just leave it on the floor with the other things that seem to have been discarded here for ages.

Dragging the mattress off the bed, I heave it through the door and down the stairs, struggling to get it into the hallway without toppling all the newspaper stacks. I'm careful but a few go flying anyway. First, I'll get the mattress into the shed, then I'll return to rebuild the towers I'd upset.

I work as fast as I can and stand back to admire my hand-iwork. At least, I should have a softer bed. Perhaps there are extra blankets, or even a duvet, somewhere in the house. En route back upstairs, I stop to tidy up the mountains of news-papers. It's not as easy as I thought at first, and I thank my height that enables me to reach the top because I can't see a ladder anywhere. How on earth did Grandfather manage it? But judging by the yellowing of the papers and their dates, they've been here a long time, so he must have done it all when he was younger and more vigorous.

I don't fancy going up those dark stairs again, but force myself, simultaneously feeling grateful I won't have to do so every day. The shed may turn out to be the better deal after all.

I scour the rooms again, going through wardrobes and cup-boards, and find thicker blankets and clean bed linen. I also grab several pillows and go to fix my bed in the shed. Now I've tidied away all the gardening stuff into a corner, the shed looks bigger and more homely. The rug in front of the bed I'd confiscated from a bedroom in the house, helps too.

I feel dusty and hungry and make my way back to the kitchen.

Grandfather's there, making toast with eggs and baked beans. He shoves a plate at me and points to drawers behind me in which I find knives and forks. Only now do I notice the stools under the table. I pull one out and make a space among the engine parts and debris on the table for my plate. Grandfather sits down opposite and without looking at me, starts eating.

I don't know if it's because I'm so hungry or because I'd grown used to the crap they served in prison, but it's the best food I've tasted in a long while.

Grandfather reads my mind and offers more food which I gratefully accept and scoff as quickly as I can.

He glances at me as he boils the kettle for coffee. His voice is raspy but not unfriendly.

"If you're gonna eat that much, you'd better earn your keep. The backyard can do with a good clearing. Then you can do the front."

I nod as the front door bell rings.

I get up.

"I'll go."

Why do all the prison services people look the same, drab, non-descript, as though they're spies, blending into the background. This guy seems okay, not austere as some of them are.

He follows me down the hall.

Grandfather is at the door leading to the living room.

He tips his chin in greeting to the man and indicates for us to go into the living room before he goes upstairs.

I move stuff off two chairs and drag them opposite each other, waiting for the officer to sit down first.

He opens his briefcase and pulls out a folder.

I don't understand half of what he says but I'm grateful for his patience.

Though he's evidently somewhat shocked at my living conditions, he appears satisfied I have somewhere to live while they find me a flat of my own. He explains about money I'll receive and a case worker who's been appointed to me and with whom I'll have regular contact.

I programme their numbers into my phone and shake his hand at the front door.

Grandmother was right - moving away from the bad influences in Liverpool was the best thing for me.

It feels as though my life is finally about to take off.

CHAPTER 20

WHERE DID THE WEEKS go?

It feels as though I've been here, living with Grandfather and sleeping in the shed, for months already. Even memories of prison are fading. Living in Liverpool with Mother and Grandmother feels like another lifetime, long ago.

I'm proud of myself for all the work I've done. The backyard looks brilliant now - a proper garden. The front needs more work, but I've managed to clear all the weeds and cut the grass.

Grandfather came to inspect it and though he only grunted, I could tell he thought I'd done a good job, too.

It's much easier to walk to the kitchen from the shed now. I no longer feel like I'm hacking my way through a jungle to get here.

I've even managed to clear the kitchen table. All Grandfather's rusty, old machine parts are now stacked in a neat pile near the door. I've given homes to the rest of the debris or thrown out what needed to go.

Grandfather was surprisingly easygoing about it and made no fuss.

He's making our usual Sunday breakfast and my stomach rumbles in anticipation as I grab a stool from under the table and plonk down on it. I've learned it's not a good idea to try to help. Grandfather doesn't like it when I get under his feet. So, I leave the cooking to him but clear up after our meals. It's a grand arrangement.

When our breakfast is nearly over, Grandfather lifts his chin at me.

"Suppose you're taking off, today bein' Sunday."

It isn't so much a question as a statement and not something I'd considered before.

It sounds a great idea but where will I go?

At once, images of London's Hyde Park I'd seen on the telly years ago, pop into my mind. It seemed the perfect park then, and I've always longed to see it for myself.

Breakfast finished, and my mind made up, I stand.

"I want to visit Hyde Park."

Grandfather gives directions to the nearest bus stop and I fetch my warmer jacket and leftover money from Grandmother.

It feels weirdly liberating walking down a road I don't know, into an unfamiliar city to a place I may have elevated in my mind to something it couldn't live up to. But it was good to feel this free, to breathe in the autumn air laden with the scent of burning leaves and grass clippings rolling over fences.

I lengthen my strides as I see a bus approaching the stop I'm aiming for. I have to run the last few steps to get to it before it leaves, but the bus driver has seen me and waits for me to jump in.

The journey to Hyde Park takes a good while but I don't mind. I'm feasting my eyes on the scenery we pass. At every stop, people get on and off and I'm fascinated by their otherness. London appears to be such a diverse place as every country on Earth seems represented, judging by the different appearances and languages.

Life in Ireland and Liverpool was pretty standard compared to London.

I'm excited by the possibilities for an extraordinary life London can offer me. What would my life be like here?

The feeling reminds me I should hear from the prison services next week about a home of my own and apparently, because of my perceived illness - which I'm guessing they believe is epilepsy - a social worker will be appointed who will also help with money and getting me some kind of work. Though what I'll do, I can't imagine. I'm not trained for anything.

Meanwhile, I want to enjoy this freedom as much as I can. I know only too well that when others are appointed to check up on you and run your life, you may as well be in prison again.

I'd asked the bus driver to let me know when we're near Hyde Park but I needn't have bothered because there's a screen at the front that announces when the bus arrives somewhere passengers want to get off. It reads, "Next stop, Hyde Park."

A wave of excitement washes over me, through me and I get up, walk to the doors that will open once we reach the stop. I'm aware I'm grinning and people are looking at me, but I don't care. It's a long time since I've experienced what happiness feels like.

I get off at the stop opposite Hyde Park and wait for the lights to change, then walk as fast as I can across the road, through the gates and into the park. It feels like I'm on holiday in an exotic country, even though in my head I know I'm still in London. The trees are bigger than I'd imagined and many are still green - probably evergreens.

I stand still, close my eyes and inhale deep lungfuls of air that feel saturated with the scents and sounds of the park - shrubs, grasses, trees, water from the Serpentine, birds, squirrels, people, dogs and food.

Music reaches me from a distance and opening my eyes, I look in its direction. I see a circle of people sitting on the lawn having a picnic, laughing, enjoying themselves. I guess the music comes from them.

Walking along the path, I'm surprised to find several statues in small clearings among the trees. But I'm heading for the Serpentine. I want to see the swans on the water.

As the water comes into view, I also see a group of strangely dressed individuals nearby in a meadow under a massive tree surrounded by bushes. They're clearly adults in stature but dressed in the costumes of animals.

I stop. What on Earth...?

At first, I wonder if it's some kind of outdoor play but soon realise they're not performing for the public. Instead, they seem wholly focussed on one another, behaving in the way their costume animal most likely would. The cats are grooming themselves, the dogs are running around, sniffing each other, the squirrels are hiding behind trees and pretend-stuffing their cheeks with nuts they find on the ground. There's even a male lion who lies in the shade on his back, paws in the air.

I try not to stare but it's hard to tear my eyes away from them, especially the blue kitten who notices me and stops cleaning its ear.

As though someone gives an invisible sign, they all stop and turn to look at me.

I want to walk away and lower my head, but a voice calls to me.

"Hey! You wanna join us?"

Before I can answer, they're around me, touching and sniffing me. I don't move.

The lion walks over and the spell is broken.

He touches my shoulder.

"Do you want to join us? We can help you with a costume, if you'd like?"

What have I got to lose?

I shrug.

"Okay. Why not. But what are you?"

The blue kitten answers, large blue eyes watching me through holes in the mask. The male voice is soft and musical.

"We're Furries, silly."

CHAPTER 21

I**T'S LATE WHEN** I get home. The front door is locked, and the only way to get to my shed is over the garage's roof. It doesn't look too high from where I'm standing, but when I slide down the rickety old pipe for the third time in my attempt to scale it, I stop to take off my Furry costume and throw it onto the roof.

It's still difficult to get up there as I'm not the slimmest or most athletic guy I know, but I manage. I have to wait a minute or two to catch my breath and drum up enough courage to jump off into the backyard on the other side. The garage roof is higher than I figured and the drop to the backyard takes my breath away. But I have no choice. Closing my eyes, I take a deep breath and jump, but can't help yelping when I land. At least I landed on grass and not the concrete path or my yelp may have included the sound of pain rather than only surprise.

Thankfully, the house stays dark.

I don't want to wake up Grandfather. I guess neither Grandfather nor I thought I'd need a key.

The prison services guy is coming in the morning to take me to my new home, so I won't need a key now.

It's the tenth night I've been out to meet up with my new buddies, the Furries.

Blue Kitten kept his word, took my measurements and arrived with a costume for me tonight. I love my costume. Cats have always been my favourite animals and my black cat costume is perfect. I don't know Blue Kitten's name or any of the others and they don't know mine. It helps with the mystery, I guess, and I don't mind. It still amazes me how brilliant my Furry friends are and how lucky I came across them.

They've given such lovely compliments about my voice, too, and I love that we meet in Hyde Park every evening to go from there on adventures. They've already shown me more of London than I'm sure I would have seen on my own in five years.

The only reason I know the big Male Lion lives quite near me is that we get the same bus back home, but he gets off before me.

It's a little weird at first, but I surprise myself with how quickly I get used to their ways. I don't find it strange now how they rub up against each other when we first meet, or the tiny white tablets everyone takes to "enhance the experience," the Green Squirrel told me in a high, fast-paced female voice. I'm sure the tablets work because I feel myself becoming a cat soon after taking them.

Tonight was interesting when Blue Kitten gave me my costume. Everyone was keen to help me get into it. The zipper that spans from the middle of my back to my navel allows me to get into the costume easily and Blue Kitten explained it's also convenient when I need the loo.

Usually, we all travel on buses or the underground together going from one place to another, but I notice from time to time, several members of our group disappearing for a while. I never notice when they reappear, but they always do. Perhaps it's something else I'll learn about in time. My heart beat faster at the thought of more Furry secrets.

I reckon tonight we were out later than usual, because Grandfather's house is already dark. I haven't got my phone with me, so I don't know the time. But I feel exhausted, so it must be late.

I stow my cat costume in my rucksack, and get into bed. My bed is so much more comfortable now and I'm aware I'm grinning from happiness as I throw my covers over me.

Life is perfect.

A N ANNOYING BANGING SOUND wakes me up and I shield my eyes against the morning sun streaming through the window. I don't have to look at my phone to know I've overslept. The phone's angry vibrating and the banging on the shed's door intensify the horrible headache thudding against my temples. I get up and unlock the door.

Grandfather's face is sour and his eyebrows are more unruly than usual.

"You're late. Your visitors are here."

He walks away while I scurry to get some clothes on and run a hand through my hair. It'll have to do.

I don't have many belongings and stuff everything into the battered old suitcase Grandmother had given me. The rest of the stuff goes into the rucksack with my cat costume.

I look around one last time, then shut the door.

The prison services guy is sitting on the sofa in the living room. An empty mug stands on the coffee table in front of him. On a chair near the window sits a man I've not seen before. His face is a little friendlier.

I look from one to the other.

"Sorry I'm late."

The new guy turns out to be Barry, my social worker.

He stands, stretches out a hand.

"Good to meet you, Lee. I'm sure we'll become great friends. Now you're here, we may as well get you to your new home."

The prison services guy leads the way to the front door, but I notice he's as wary of the newspaper mountains as I was.

Grandfather nods at me. It looks like his watery blue eyes are more watery than usual, but I'm probably just seeing things.

I shift my rucksack and touch his arm.

"Thanks for everything, Grandpa. I'll come see you soon."

Barry shakes Grandfather's hand and asks if he wants to come along to view my new home. Apparently, it's not far away.

Grandfather grunts and shuts the front door.

We walk down the path to a parked car near the gate. The front garden looks grand now. I've cleared away all the dead plants and weeds and re-arranged the paving slabs so the path doesn't look dilapidated anymore.

I feel proud of my handiwork, but don't brag about it to them. It's enough that Grandfather gave me a thumbs-up when he came to inspect my achievements.

I get in the back of the car, put my stuff at my feet. Barry wasn't wrong. The journey from Grandfather's house to my flat takes twenty minutes. I could probably walk to see him.

My flat is in a brand new block. We walk up the stairs to my flat, the only one of six.

Barry unlocks the door and I go inside to put my stuff down near the wall. It's small, but it's mine.

The prison services guy follows me.

"You won't need anything. Everything you want is here."

He shows me the TV mounted on the wall, a brown chair and sofa nearby, and opens the kitchen cupboards that contain several plates, mugs and glasses. Two tall stools sit under the breakfast bar that forms part of the kitchenette.

Barry follows us.

The sofa is a pull-out bed, and the bedding is in the cupboard.

The prison services guy shows me where everything is kept, and I marvel at the space-saving gadgets. It's the nicest, most modern flat I've ever seen.

The men don't stay. They shake my hand at the front door and I watch them disappear down the stairs.

Turning back into the flat and closing the door, I can hardly believe it's my home now.

In the kitchenette, I pour myself a glass of water and switch on the telly. It's been so long since I've watched anything. Surfing through the channels, I find an episode of Midsummer Murders, one of my favourites. For what feels like the millionth time, I'm wondering what Grandfather does without a TV. It appears he is reading newspapers.

As I laugh at my joke, my stomach growls and I realise I've eaten nothing since last night.

Barry told me there was a good corner shop nearby where I could buy food and even a beer if I wanted. I'm counting my money. I must be mindful of what I have left since it's not much, but Barry said he was trying to arrange something for me with a Government grant or something like it. To be honest, I wasn't really listening. My attention was on my lovely little flat.

I grab my money and head outside, wondering what I can get to eat straight away, as I don't want to cook anything. I'm too hungry.

The corner shop is bigger than I'd expected and they have everything I could want. I grab biscuits, crisps, a sandwich and a packet of beers. One sandwich won't cut it, I'm famished. I glance around to see if anyone is looking and quickly put a few more sandwiches in my jacket.

No one stops me and I'm happy to pay for the rest. But watching my money disappear as I buy the stuff makes me feel panicky.

The shop doesn't have a security alarm and I leave easily.

Walking home, I cross my fingers Barry will arrange something soon. I don't even have enough money to get into London tonight to meet up with the Furries. But I don't mind. Spending my first night on my own in my new flat will be a grand adventure. I have food, a telly and a soft sofa. What more could I want?

I know I'll be happy here.

CHAPTER 22

I've become quite adept at carrying my Furry costume in a way that makes it look like some kind of rucksack. It means I have nothing extra to carry once I put it on. The shirt fits me with lots of room, but it's been getting slightly snug around my waist lately. It must be all the biscuits I've taken from the corner shop.

The girl with the blonde ponytail saw me the other day and tried to stop me, but I just walked out as if nothing was under my jacket. Barry got me some money, but it's not enough, and he said he was working on getting me more.

I'm saving as much as possible to meet up with the Furries. Otherwise, I'm afraid I'll lose contact with them and be lonely again. They're my first friends in London, and I like that they just accepted me knowing nothing about me. It makes me feel normal. Even the Glome likes them, I can tell. He loves it when we go on adventures, and I can feel him vibrating with excitement inside me. But he's been quiet since we came to London, and I'm grateful he's not scaring my new friends.

Tonight, we're "hunting," as The Lion calls it. We're deliberately targeting people we feel would be good to add to our numbers. But I'm not sure I want to take part in the "hunting" because I don't like to thrust myself at strangers the way my Furry friends appear to relish.

"Come on, Black Cat," The Lion says in my ear and pushes me towards a beautiful man in his late twenties.

"He's looking at you. He's ready to be 'hunted.' Just do it."

The Lion pushes me harder, and I collide with the man. His eyes widen as I grab his shoulders, but I don't think he's scared. He seems intrigued. He's not the only one.

Inside me, the Glome is vibrating with anticipation and excitement. I can't fight him as he surfaces, his voice flowing through me.

"Why don't you join us? You'll have such fun."

Everyone, including the man, stops and stares at me.

I'm fighting to keep the Glome contained, but now he's emerged, he has no intention of disappearing again. He wants to join us and uses my voice to mesmerise everyone around me. Since I can't fight him, I allow him free rein and watch how he charms and bamboozles everyone. By the end of the night, I count six new members to our Furry tribe. I'm not sure I like it. It was better with only the seven of us. Why would we need new members, and who decided it? No one told me we were going to "hunt" tonight. I didn't even know it was a thing, and I hope we don't do it too often.

The Glome finally notices I'm unhappy with the situation and retreats to comfort me. Thankfully, simultaneously, the "hunting" stops. But I'm taken aback by the behaviour of the Furries I'd come to know over the past few months. Usually, I see nothing weird about how they rub against each other and even me. Tonight feels different, though. I can feel a strange energy, like an electric current running through them. It's unusual, but not uncomfortable. The new recruits walk with us back to Hyde Park. It becomes darker as we walk further into the trees, away from the lights of the road and the city.

Blue Kitten flirts with the beautiful guy, our first recruit of the night. To my surprise, the guy responds, grabbing Blue Kitten's face and kissing his mouth. The two disappear off into the trees. No one else seems to notice because they're all busy playing with each other and the rest of the new recruits. One of them, a big guy, yanks me towards him and pulls me by my hand behind a huge, old oak tree. He pushes me over and fumbles behind me with my zipper.

I'm frozen. It reminds me of that time in prison with Ned, and I realise it's no different this time. Icy cold washes over me as I remember the Glome's response to Ned. There's no mistaking what this big guy wants and I almost feel sorry for him, he doesn't know about the Glome, what the Glome can do. Will the Glome repeat the same scenario as last time with Ned?

But the Glome remains silent. I can feel him, of course, but he's waiting, watching and I wonder if I'm imagining it, because I'm almost positive the Glome is enjoying himself. I've never felt this energy from him before. Why is this happening?

A weird feeling washes over me that the Glome has orchestrated this. The evidence of his voice on people has long been a source of amazement and strange power that I enjoyed, that I pretended was my own. But it never occurred to me that the Glome could make people do his bidding in other, less obvious ways. Is he using mind control? I've always known my life wasn't my own, that I was in his control. But it never occurred to me he might control those around me, too.

My hand shakes from fear, from the enormity of my epiphany, as I find the zipper at my navel and pull open the suit.

The guy pushes my tracksuit bottoms down, and I feel him touching me, arousing me before he enters me. He groans in my ear as he does so. Another reminder of Ned and, for moments, the shower at the prison, flashes through my mind's eye.

I'm appalled that the Glome is silent. None of his usual fury rises in me. But I'm grateful for not having to fight him, too, because what's happening to me now feels more than surreal. I see myself as from above being assaulted by the guy. I feel nothing. Have I pushed my emotions down into my body so much that abominable events like these now leave me numb?

It's over sooner than I thought. The man pushes me straight up against the tree. His voice is hoarse and low.

"This is what you Furries like, is it? I had no idea. Great to meet you, man. Can't wait to spend more time with you."

I'm shocked.

What?

In all the months I'd been with the Furries, I'd never thought about anything sexual. But all those times some of them disappeared, strikes me. Perhaps that's what they were doing, then? But I'm also pretty sure some of my Furry friends aren't here for anything sexual. Rather, like me, they're here for companionship, friendship and something to do with people who accept you for who you are. It makes me wonder if they're as lonely as I am. I guess so.

The guy takes my hand and leads me back to the group, where several Furries are still sexually engaged with partners.

I don't know where to look, but can't tear my eyes from them. I know also that part of my inability to look away is because the Glome is enjoying it.

How did I not know this part of the Furries?

The costumes take on a whole new meaning for me now, and I see how every costume is its wearer's sexual orientation and preference. Guess I'm the stray cat. But something about me must have given away my innermost thoughts and fears to Blue Kitten, who'd created the perfect costume for me.

Now it's all out in the open, I feel calm. The earlier weird energy of the group makes complete sense.

The Lion makes me jump when he suddenly appears at my side.

"Love full moons, don't you?"

He points up at the moon, and only now do I realise he's right. A massive yellow orb rises above the treetops. It's a full moon tonight.

I'm aware of the Glome's satisfied sigh inside me.

CHAPTER 23

J AMES MUST HAVE PICKED up my thoughts because his stunning voice reverberates in my mind.

"You're right, Lee. Nothing can exist outside the Consciousness, which is Love. Nothing. Even darkness is part of it."

Wait.

Does James know about the Glome? Do the others? No one has said anything or hinted that they're aware of it. But James's words seem to imply he knows about the Glome.

But there's no judgement in his energy, and I feel no condemnation from the others either.

Perhaps trying to hide my thoughts about the Glome from them has been futile. There can be no secrets here. I understand it now. Not here, where the Love opens everything, where viewing our experiences and opportunities to learn and expand is the focus.

I decide not to bury my thoughts about the Glome any longer since everything about it is probably already clear to my soul tribe.

I turn to James.

"When you say even the darkness is part of Consciousness, do you also mean the darkness that lived inside me in my physical form?"

Again, James's energy momentarily brightens.

"Indeed, I do, Lee. It's something none of us ever dared to do. But you chose it for all of us, for all of Consciousness to discover that experience."

I'd be shocked by his words if I could.

"None of you ever chose it? Why in Love's name did I do it? What madness possessed me? It's been awful to deal with, as if my physical life wasn't difficult enough."

James's energy blazes for moments.

"Not madness, Lee. You were brave. It's rare that fragments of Consciousness choose the path you did. The value is vital for a swifter expansion for all than could otherwise happen."

I notice the other souls in my tribe have all taken on a similar light energy to James's, though theirs are less bright.

"Why didn't anyone stop me? You were all there when I made that crazy decision. Did you all think it was a good idea?"

The silence that follows makes me wonder if I've overstepped the mark with my question.

I soon realise it's space left for me to examine my question instead. But how can I dissect it without more information?

I feel, rather than see, James's presence beside me.

"Your decision to allow a fragment of darkness to accompany your physical life was something we discussed at length, Lee. Souls rarely choose that path."

"Then why did I?"

Another energy appears beside me. It's the girl with the golden curls who was Mother. But now even the golden curls are gone, and only the true, pure essence of the soul remains. I understand at once that she is indeed what the others referred to as an ascended master. Her energy is light and effervescent.

"You have a unique path, Lee. Your essence is intertwined with that of the energy you know as James. Sometimes, fragments splinter further, and that's what the energy known as James did with you.

"You must have recognised each other when you met in physical form and felt an affinity with him, yes? Perhaps you even understood it through the beauty of your voices? As you know, the voice is that part of your soul that speaks directly to the physical world, so others can hear your soul and resonate with you."

She's obviously telling the truth. I sense it.

When I first encountered James, I felt it. His voice was what I heard first, and then I saw the fire for life in his blue eyes. His energy was wild, most likely made more so by the drugs he'd been taking that night. But I felt myself respond to him in a way I never had with anyone else, though I didn't know what it meant. I do now.

Yes, she speaks the truth. James and I are two sides of one energy.

The Mother energy flares again.

"Not two sides of the same energy, dear Lee. James has shared himself with one other. She's not here with us right now. But you may remember her?"

Again, I'm surrounded by silence and understand it's their way of allowing me the space to absorb what's being revealed.

Things are falling into place for me. I do remember… Isabelle. Her voice drew me in and I trusted her at once. On some level, I must have known we three were parts of the same fragment of Consciousness.

Meeting people like James and Isabelle, was extraordinary. We were worlds apart in our physical lives, and unless pre-planned in the non-physical, I don't see how our paths could ever have crossed. On that fateful night, I remember feeling it was surreal because they were both unique, even in their physical forms.

James is beyond amazing here. His gradual transformation is alarming, but fascinating. As a fragment of James, I wonder what's in store for me.

James's energy flashes momentarily before his voice fills my mind, far more beautiful than before.

"You don't have to wonder, Lee. We're all gathered here to witness your transformation."

I look down at myself, but I'm the same as everyone else.

What can James mean, '*my* transformation?' I thought we could all see *his* transformation. And what does it have to do with the Glome?

So, not all has been revealed yet. I'm trepidatious about what more I'll learn, but excited too.

CHAPTER 24

I T'S LIKE THE FULL moon has crazed my Furry friends and everyone else around us.

I've never seen the streets so busy so late at night. People are dancing, drinking, laughing and having an amazing time. Their high energy is infectious. Everyone loves our costumes when we join in the fun.

I guess I'm being poked and prodded to figure out who's disguised as me.

It tickles so much that I can't help but giggle.

We all pile onto the bus, still laughing. I need to find a seat and go towards the rear of the bus, so I can more comfortably fit in a double seat. Several Furries, including the Male Lion and a few new friends, follow me and take up most of the spaces and seats. We're in high spirits, and the drink being passed around also helps to further our mirth. I was meant to take my meds ages ago, but the drinking and sitting are helping to ground me somewhat.

Can't believe I left the stuff at home. If I could get a cigarette, it would help me even more. But smoking on the bus isn't allowed, and I don't even have ciggies on me.

The Furries and our new recruits are making friends with others around us. I'm irritated by all the "friendliness."

Perhaps my Furry friends read my energy because Male Lion slaps my back.

"Hey man, why so quiet?"

Before I can respond, two very rowdy guys board the bus and head for us. They're either drunk or high or both. At first, their antics seem harmless. They pull Male Lion's tail and poke Green Squirrel's cheeks.

The shorter of the two brings his face close to Blue Kitten's mask.

"And what might you be? Who are you hiding inside there, huh?"

We're all stunned when he leans back and spits in Blue Kitten's eyes

Blue Kitten is yowling and clawing at his mask, desperate to get it off.

I wonder what substances coat the guy's spit that's now burning Blue Kitten's eyes.

Male Lion jumps up to help get the goo out of Blue Kitten's eyes while addressing the spitter.

His brown eyes are blazing from his mask.

"What the fuck is the matter with you, you moron!"

The two drunk guys snicker and spit again, this time on the floor, barely missing Male Lion's once-white trainers.

The change in energy is immediate and disturbing. No one laughs, and our jollity disappears like smoke in the wind. A sudden menace infiltrated the bus.

It becomes clear the two drunk men are part of a larger group that surrounds us. Their presence appears to give the short guy more confidence.

Short Spitter Guy's face distorts with rage.

His voice slices through his spittle that flies everywhere.

"What's wrong with you people? You're a disgrace to humanity. Playing make-believe and dressing like children's toys when you're adults. You make me sick, you do. Probably all paedos, ain't ye, the lot of yous."

He spits again, and I notice green strings in the glistening phlegm.

The rest of their crowd joins in the chant he starts.

"Paedos! Paedos! Paedos!"

Short Guy pushes Green Squirrel's chest. He screams to be heard.

"Oh, lookie here! This one's a girl. A girl paedo. Rare breed, I'd say."

He's laughing, turning his face to his mates, who're all nodding and jeering, pointing at us, continuing their ridiculous chant.

Short Guy turns back to Green Squirrel and pushes her harder, so she falls backwards on top of an elderly gentleman sitting on his own reading a book.

She tries to get away from the older man, apologising to him. But Short Guy grabs her by the forearms and headbutts her, so she falls down on top of the older man again.

The older man stares at Short Guy over glasses balanced on his nose.

I'll never know if he was going to say something to Short Guy because something in the older man's gaze must trigger something in Short Guy.

He goes berserk, screaming and yelling at the older man.

"What you looking at, hey? Mind your own goddamn business and stay out of mine, always interfering where you're not wanted, you stupid old fucker! You're everywhere, ain't ye? Lurking, lurking, watching, judging. Everywhere. Everywhere I turn, there you are with your pathetic face, smelling like piss. Why don't you piss off? Go on! Piss off."

Short Guy's body carries danger as he leans towards the older man. Green Squirrel is still flung over his lap. Both are frozen as Short Guy gets closer and raises his fist. Everyone is quiet, watching. Two of Short Guy's friends approach him, wanting to contain the situation before things get out of hand.

His taller friend, who first got on the bus with him, touches his shoulder.

"Come on, man. He's a stranger. Let's just go."

But Short Guy shrugs off his friend's hand and puts up both fists, ready to strike. It's difficult for him to keep his balance as the bus drives over bumps in the road and around corners. I reckon the drink, drugs, or whatever else in his system also accounts for his inability to stay steady.

Without warning, Short Guy punches Green Squirrel instead. We all hear the crunch of her bones as he breaks her nose and the following scream.

Short Guy's friends grab him as the bus stops and try to drag him away. But he resists.

Then, everything happens quickly. Male Lion moves like lightning, and I barely see the glint of the blade in his hand as he thrusts at Short Guy's stomach with it.

Short Guy's friends push him off the bus, but he collapses at the bus stop. Only two of his friends stay with him while the others holler, scream, and shout as they run into the night.

I don't think they saw the stabbing or realise how seriously Short Guy's been wounded.

Male Lion is pulling Green Squirrel to her feet, apologising to the older man and shouting for us all to follow him as he jumps from the bus.

I can't move fast enough, and before I even reach the doors, they've closed, and the bus has taken off again. I watch my friends through the doors, wondering how quickly I can re-join them, trying to familiarise myself with where they'd disembarked. My memory isn't great, and I pray I can remember the way back to them.

I don't return to my seat, standing instead and holding on to the bar, ready to get off at the next stop.

Though everyone is quiet and shocked, the bus driver is talking loudly on his phone, but I can't hear what he's saying. The sound of his voice is comforting, however.

Only the front door opens when the bus stops at the next stop. Standing, I wait a bit to see if the doors where I'm standing will open, but they remain closed. I'm about to get off at the front, but two policemen appear.

I stop.

Shit. I can't be in trouble again.

The moment the policemen are on board, the front door closes.

The ginger-haired policeman speaks loud enough for everyone to hear.

"Stay where you are. There's been a serious incident, and we want to talk to everyone. If a seat is available, sit."

I return to the double seats I'd vacated and sit down again. May as well wait my turn. There's not much I can tell them. But the sight of the blade in Male Lion's hand sticks in my mind.

I watch as the policemen talk to everyone and approach me. I'm aware my breathing has increased, and I suddenly feel far too hot in my costume, but I know I can't take it off.

The Greek-looking police officer approaches me.

"You were with a group of people wearing animal costumes like yours?"

My head appears to bob without my consent.

The policeman has a small book in his hand where he makes notes.

"Why didn't you leave with them?"

I shrug. What can I say? That I'm too large to move fast? Surely, he can see that for himself, but I realise I must speak. Otherwise, I may get into trouble.

"The doors closed before I could get off with them. I wanted to get off here and walk back to meet them."

The ginger-haired officer joins us.

"Where were you all going?"

What can I say? How can I convince the policemen I don't have a clue?

"I'm not sure. I was just tagging along with them."

The Greek officer looks up from his book.

"Do you live nearby?"

"Yes."

"And where do they live?"

"I don't know. I was just following along."

The officers glance at each other before the Greek officer continues.

"Right. The other passengers have confirmed you were with a group of people dressed like you. So, those people are your friends, right?"

My head bobs again.

"If they're your friends, why would they leave you on the bus alone?"

My heart is doing a drum solo in my neck. I know this tone only too well.

I'm grateful when the Glome takes over and the richer sounds of my voice flow out of me.

"One of my friends got injured when a guy hit her in the face, and they got off to get her help, I guess."

The police officers stare at me, and I read in their eyes their astonishment at the beauty of my voice. I know that other passengers nearby are also openly gazing at me. If they're this impressed with my voice while I'm wearing my costume, I can only imagine how impressed they'd be when they meet me without it. Haven't I seen it enough? The fat boy with the ugly scar on his cheek having the audacity to speak with such a stunning, musical voice? Surely, it's an outrage.

The Greek police officer shakes his head as though he's shaking off the stupor in which the Glome always casts its listeners. My respect for him raises significantly because I've seen how effective the Glome's mesmerising abilities are. The officer signals to the bus driver, who opens the doors near us. The officer shows he wants me to disembark.

I know I'm in trouble, but I'm not sure why, and the knowledge makes me move slower than usual. But neither officer hurries me. They appear patient as they allow me to get off before them.

Outside on the pavement, the ginger officer speaks into his radio. I can't help overhearing he's calling for a van to collect us.

My entire body sags.

Here we go again. How in the hell do I get myself into these serious situations with no fault of my own? Do I just have some weird writing on my forehead or something?

I don't resist when they cuff me and shove me into the van that arrives within minutes. They're not rough with me, though, and I have hope they'll cut me loose when we get to the station, and I have to give a statement.

I DON'T KNOW WHAT time it is, but I must have been here for hours already. The costume is itching me, even though I've removed the head part that Blue Kitten had thoughtfully velcroed to the body so it was easy to detach. I'm hot, hungry, beyond exhausted, and I need my meds.

But they haven't finished with me yet. Asking the same questions, getting the same replies.

I don't bloody know who these people in Furry costumes are. Why won't they believe me?

CHAPTER 25

I LOOK DOWN AT myself and realise I'm less dense than before, not quite as diaphanous or as bright as those around me, but it's clear the transformation they talked about has begun.

It's the second time I've experienced this kind of tightening panic, though time doesn't exist here and I no longer have a physical body. So, how is it possible? Is it a foreshadowing of what's happening to me? What am I becoming? Does the Glome play any part in it?

Beside me, James's energy flares momentarily.

"We advise you to look first at your own life, understand what you were trying to achieve, and whether you feel satisfied. Then, if you still want to, we can look at the Glome, as you called it."

I get the impression he's being cautious, which only serves to intensify my feeling that the Glome is more important than I ever imagined. The idea disturbs me.

I direct my thoughts at him.

"How much more is there to watch?"

I can feel his smile.

"It's like a movie. Watch until the end."

The warmth of the others surrounding me expands. I feel their excitement, curiosity, and patience.

It's odd that even though their bodies have changed and I can no longer recognise them that way, I still feel their personalities and energy as though I can see them, like before.

A slight brightening in the being that identified earlier as the older man with long white hair and a beard, alerts me he's directing his thoughts to me.

"James is right. It's important you understand what you've achieved, not just for yourself, but for all of us, including James."

What?

I turn towards James.

"Was meeting you part of a bigger pre-planned life? I thought because I'm a fragment of you, we had to meet so you could leave your physical body in the way you did. Wasn't it all that was agreed?"

Again, James's energy flares brighter for a moment.

"That was only a small part of it, Lee. You're right, there's a far bigger, more important reason behind what we'd agreed."

Around us, the others' energy brightens and brightens in anticipation, as though this was the part of my story they'd been waiting for all along.

I feel hemmed in somehow and move away, but James and the others follow me and form a circle around me again, as though they're protecting me. I don't want to think they're shielding me from the Glome but understand it's a possibility. Something about the Glome is going to be revealed soon. I can feel it and it makes me more nervous and simultaneously also impatient. But I'll follow their advice and watch my life unfold.

As though James understands my frustration, his energy flares again before his thoughts reach me.

"Like you, I had made my physical life as challenging as I could, Lee. You see, I wanted to stop myself from having to go back repeatedly... stop reincarnation."

I'm amazed. It never occurred to me we reincarnated over and over again. But now James has mentioned it, it makes complete sense. Otherwise, how would we learn and evolve and grow together as one Consciousness if we never reincarnated? How odd I never considered it before. To stop it, however... That would be something, yet I'm unsure how.

James's thoughts continue to sing through my mind.

"There are several ways to stop reincarnating and I wanted to choose one I knew would bring me everlasting joy. But it's complicated and almost no one ever chooses it because it involves so many variables that can go wrong."

Curiosity spikes in my energy. I'm aware of everyone's soft, scintillating laughter surrounding me. They're not laughing at me, however, but sharing in my enthusiasm to discover the mystery behind James's statement. Though I realise they already know it and are only enjoying my reaction to it.

This time, when James's thoughts reach me, I'm aware his sound has changed again. Even more melodious, with more layers of harmonics than ever before.

So, either my hearing has changed or his transformation is continuing, too.

The many rainbow sounds run through my mind again as everyone enjoys that thought.

The energy of the woman with the fiery mane blazes for moments before her thoughts reach me.

"We're all continuing to transform and evolve all the time, dear Lee. There's no limit and no end to it."

It sounds exhausting to me.

No sooner did those words enter my thoughts, than the effervescent rainbow sounds run through me again as everyone laughs at what they feel is my joke. Exhaustion doesn't exist here.

But when James's energy flashes momentarily, everyone's vibration changes and I'm certain the revelations are about to begin.

James's thoughts are like a gentle breeze soothing me at once.

"First, thank you, Lee. Without you, I wouldn't have been able to achieve my goals. You had to agree to it because it coloured your life drastically, on top of the challenges you sought for yourself."

A thought I can't shake forms inside me.

"Wait. Before you tell me more, I must ask something first. If I'm your fragment, how many lives have I had before now, and was this my last? How did you split us and what will happen to me now?"

Again, the sparkling, rainbow sounds of the others' laughter flow through me.

The essence of the young girl brightens. Then her bell-like thoughts penetrate me.

"So many questions, Lee. Don't worry, everything will be explained in steps that make sense to you. Patience is a good quality to have, even here. But trust is the most important. Just trust that everything will be revealed when it's the right moment to do so. All your questions will be answered, but perhaps not in the way you expect. So, trust, dear Lee."

As though I'm suddenly far smarter here, I grasp her meaning at once and relax.

I turn back to James and wait for him to continue.

His energy brightens again, and then his thoughts ripple through me.

"What you've done is extremely important, Lee. You may not remember it all now, but you will do so soon. Meanwhile, thank you for helping not only me but all of humanity."

I'd gasp if I could.

The idea of 'all of humanity' sounds so far out of my comfort zone or my ability to affect, almost grandiose. In my physical body, my reaction may have been vastly different. Here, I feel calm when I'm sure I'd have been overwhelmed in the physical. But I understand trust, and I trust James.

He continues even though I know my thoughts reached him.

"My purpose for my life was to affect humanity as much as I could using love. It started with my human life and because I was successful, in no small part thanks to you, Lee, I can now reach my full potential here, where it matters most. The darkness you called the Glome wasn't a fluke or an accident. It's a powerful, transformative force that was carefully placed within you as I requested and with your permission."

Scenes from my life with the Glome flash before my eyes.

"But why?"

A moment's silence allows me to understand the importance of the truth to come.

James's energy vibrates faster as he moves in front of me.

"What do you know of Angels, Lee?"

CHAPTER 26

I'M BEYOND EXHAUSTED AS I wait for the bus. Sleep hasn't been my friend over the last three years and I was way too worked-up and nervous to sleep last night, knowing I'm being released today. It happens every time I'm on the verge of a life-changing situation, and let's face it, there have been a few. I mean, what are the chances of being jailed twice in my life for things I didn't even do? So, three more bloody years behind bars.

My stomach still feels tight with anxiety, but I've been focussing on the people around me, which has had a calming effect on me.

It's late and London's party-goers mill around me as they too wait for buses to take them home from the clubs that are now closed. I don't have a watch but know it's past three am because I heard someone say it. Some people, in bubbles of their own, are kissing and holding on to each other. Tomorrow, they'll wake up in rooms they don't recognise with partners they don't remember meeting as the fog of drink and drugs lift from their bodies and minds.

The noise is overwhelming, but I'm grateful for it. It's surreal, as though three years ago, I left a life I could relate to when I entered prison for the second time in my life, and tonight, after my release, I've been thrown back into a life I hardly recognise. It's exciting though, and I can't wait for normality to return. Time will tell how long I'll take to adjust this time.

When I left the prison, they returned my clothes, which I was relieved to find still fit. I didn't want the Furry costume anymore and dumped it in the nearest trashcan I could find. Why think of the injustice of the last three years?

Though I received meds in jail, I'd run out and I can feel the beginning of the restlessness that pre-warns of either an episode or violence to come. I pray it's the former.

The blue plastic bag with a pack of six beers I bought with the money I found in my pocket feels heavy. The drink helps. I didn't have enough for ciggies though, and they would have helped.

As I down my second beer, I watch the people around me. No one pays me much attention and I don't blame them. I'm not being friendly and I'm too focussed on what's happening with my body. Apart from needing meds, my tooth is giving me jip again. I must remember my appointment the nurse at the prison had made for me. The dentist there had a look but said I needed a private dentist as he didn't have the right equipment for the job and doubted an NHS dentist could tackle it.

I bag the empty beer can and grab another. But just as I open it, a man with amazing blue eyes appears before me. Out of all the people in the crowd, somehow he picks me.

But I know that look in his eyes and wonder if the drugs he's taken will help me until I can get home to my meds. I hope they're still there and will work after three years.

What wallops me is the man's astonishing voice. I've never heard such stunning lyricism in another voice, except my own when the Glome uses it. The beauty the Glome's manipulation of my vocal cords achieves, always catches me off-guard. But this guy's voice is on another level.

I'm so focussed on the sound, I almost don't hear what he says as he introduces himself.

"James."

I go to shake his hand. But he envelops me in a lovely hug. It's been such a long time since anyone had hugged me like this. I feel his goodness, and a massive sense of belonging descends on me as he holds me to him for moments longer than I imagined. My staggering emotions bring tears. Blinking them away, I try to focus on the people I can see over his shoulder. It lessens the overwhelming nameless feelings that shudder through my body.

A beautiful woman talks to two taller men and I feel they must be James's friends. The woman, especially, carries the same energy as James. When he breaks free from me and turns to introduce them, I'm relieved I'm right. At least, relief is an emotion I understand and can name.

I can tell Isabelle is a kindly woman, and she looks a bit like Mary with her dark hair arranged on top of her head. James and Isabelle had apparently come across the American couple in a club earlier that evening. The Americans gush about their trip of a lifetime to India. Now they're waiting for a plane to take them to the Burning Man Festival. The long delay in London means they can explore the city a little before returning to Heathrow for their flight in the morning. Their lives sound a million miles from mine.

James touches my shoulder.

"You want to join us? We're walking up the road to get the bus back to my place."

I'm worried about my meds. But perhaps James's drugs will help me out meanwhile, and perhaps I could borrow money from him for ciggies.

"Sure. Okay."

James turns to the Americans and leads the way further up the road where fewer people surround us.

Isabelle walks beside me.

Her voice, as musical as James's, washes through me.

"How long have you known James?"

She must see the surprise in my eyes as I stop to face her.

"I've only just met him. Weird how he just came up to hug me and invite me to join you guys. I'm not sure how long I can stay, though, because I have a dental appointment tomorrow near my home. It's with a private dentist. My brother said he'd pay for it, so I mustn't miss it. How far is James's house from here?"

I can't read the expression in Isabelle's eyes. But I see her thoughts swirling around in her head.

Her voice is stunning when she speaks again, but carries clear notes of her emotional disturbance and I focus on it instead. I wonder if she and James might be singers.

"Oh, I see. Well, I've never been to James's apartment from here, so I don't know how long it will take. But we're near the

Thames, and he lives South, so probably not long, depending on the bus."

As I watch Isabelle, I see her looking at the scar on my left cheek, her eyes narrowed and distant. But before I can ask what she's thinking, James appears at my side.

The Americans are several buildings ahead of us, though James doesn't seem in a hurry to catch up to them. But Isabelle walks towards them, leaving James and me to dawdle behind everyone.

"So, Lee, what's your story? You look all alone in the world."

I shrug and tell him I've just been released from a three-year stint in the Clink.

He doesn't seem surprised.

"Yeah, it happens to the best of us. I've been inside a few times too, but never longer than a month. And what a mistake that was. I should never have been there in the first place, a case of mistaken identity. Imagine... I got caught for driving without insurance. I don't even have a car or a licence, for god's sake. It was some other idiot with the same name as mine. But you know, once you make a fuss, you're in the wrong automatically."

I'm relieved James understands, doesn't judge me, and has had a similar experience. The injustice of being imprisoned when I wasn't the one who did the stabbing still stings my heart.

James stops suddenly and crouches down as he puts his rucksack on the pavement and rummages in it. He lifts out a small packet and pops a tablet out of the foil, puts it in his mouth.

He looks up and holds out the packet to me.

"Want one?"

I take it.

"Sure."

I push out a tablet from the foil and drink it down with the remainder of my beer. James turns down the can I offer him.

Good, more for me.

We continue walking and talking and I learn that despite him being a Highlander and me Irish, our childhoods were remarkably similar. I count my blessings I didn't have a stepdad like him, who beat the crap out of him for being gay, though.

I only notice the Americans and Isabelle again when they stop to ask how far we still have to go.

James laughs. The warmth of the sound reverberates through me.

"You'll see it. It's the next bus stop along this road. Just keep going."

I don't laugh. I'm knackered, and when I agreed to come with James, I didn't know I'd have to walk this far. But James swings his rucksack from his shoulder again and offers me another one of his tablets.

I take the packet, but I can't read what it says on there.

"What kind of drug is it?"

James takes the packet from me and pops out a tablet, holding it in his hand for me to take.

"These are my new antidepressants. They're strong and will help you feel better soon. You'll see."

I'm happy James understands what I'm going through, take the tablet and open another can of beer, my last, swallow it down fast. I felt nothing from the first tablet yet. Maybe this one will help because I'm even more jittery now and beginning to think I've made the wrong decision to come with James.

"I've just come out of jail, man. This is very far for me to walk. Can't we just take a cab?"

The Americans are much closer having waited for us to catch up to them.

The taller man with short blonde hair squints at me.

"Well, darling, you could certainly do with more walking. So, stop complaining and pick up those knees."

No one laughs, but no one defends me, either, not even the Glome. Where the hell is he when I need him?

I glare at the American but address James.

"Don't you have ciggies on you? It will help me out a lot."

The other American sniffs.

"Oh, not smoking as well. You should look after your body, you know. You only have this one and if you wear it out, where will you be then?"

I ignore them both and continue staring at James, willing him to help me. But he's too high, I can see that.

He laughs and claps me on the back.

"Do I look like someone who smokes, Lee? Come on, we're nearly there and you can buy some cigarettes at the all-night corner shop near my place."

I'm annoyed James doesn't appear to understand the severity of my situation when he seemed to do so moments ago. But I'm relieved I'll get ciggies. I hope he has money on him.

The bus arrives and I make for the double seats at the back. The Americans fly up the stairs to see London.

I catch James staring at the scar on my left cheek, just like Isabelle did earlier.

"I went to a psychic recently. She said an Irish guy with a scar on his left cheek would lead to my death. Might she have meant you, dear Lee?"

CHAPTER 27

I'M GETTING MORE AND more irritated that the bus is taking forever. I've never known a route with so many stops.

James and Isabelle are singing and though it's genuinely beautiful, I would appreciate it more if I weren't also dealing with the jitters. I wish they would stop.

The passengers on the bus applaud when they finish their song and James scrambles up the stairs to alert the Americans we're almost at his place. When the bus stops again, the three of them run down the stairs and through the doors. Isabelle follows them.

For a moment, I'm reminded of the last time I was on a bus with friends who sprinted through the doors and left me behind. Fear tightens my stomach. But I move fast and make it just in time, aware I'm sweating and shaking, as the doors hiss closed behind me.

An abandoned shopping trolley stands propped against the bus stop. The Americans grab it, pretending to dance with it, singing out-of-tune musical theatre songs. James and Isabelle climb inside the trolley, and the Americans run with it across the road, through the car park towards the shop to which it seems to belong.

I'm royally pissed off. Not only have I made a huge mistake coming with them, but I have no clue where I am, or how to get home from here. Their laughter and screams are doing my head in. I don't want to follow them, but I do so because there's no other choice.

James finally gets out of the trolley and I grab his arm.

"Hey man, do you have money for ciggies? I really need them. My jitters are getting worse and my meds are at home."

James claps me on the back.

"Isabelle will have some. Let's ask her. Which meds do you have to take for what jitters?"

We walk towards Isabelle and James seems suddenly soberer.

"Would the stuff I gave you have a detrimental effect on you?"

I'm not entirely sure what detrimental means, but I get his point.

"I don't know. My diagnosis is for epilepsy, but I feel it's something more. The meds work, so I don't care. I just know I need ciggies and a drink when I get the jitters and can't have my meds."

James leaves me for moments as he gets the money from Isabelle, who gives it, no questions asked, though her eyes flit from him to me and back again.

James stuffs a tenner in my hand.

"The all-night shop just up the road sells alcohol and ciga-rettes. We'll catch you up. It's on the way to my place, anyway."

I lift a hand in thanks to Isabelle and walk as fast as possible back through the car park towards the road. A little distance away, the shop's lights spill out through its door onto the pavement, and I see people going in and out. I head towards it.

The shop is small, but James was right about the booze and ciggies. I'm hungry too and pick up some chocolate biscuits. But the tenner doesn't go far. I need the ciggies and beer and I hide the biscuits under my jacket because I can't pay for them. I grab a large pack of beers, a lighter and tell the cashier which cigarettes I want as I pay and leave quickly.

A large, dark building opposite, has the perfect alcoved doorway. I make my way there and sit down on the cold steps. My hands are shaking when I open the first can of beer and light a ciggie. I draw the smoke into my lungs and I feel the tightness in my stomach and chest evaporate and my body relaxes. Closing my eyes, I lean my head against the wall beside me.

It's quiet. I like it. I can't hear the noise from James and his friends here. The night has swallowed me, giving me safety against the ugliness others impose on my life.

I'm not sure how long I've been sitting here, but when I finish the ciggie, James slides onto the step beside me.

"Here you are. We were wondering where you got to. Let's go to my place now."

He gets up and waits for me to collect my things. I notice he's split his jeans that now hang in shreds on either side of his muscled legs.

I stub the end of the ciggie out on the wall and follow him up the road, where Isabelle and the Americans are waiting. It's hard to ignore how out of place she appears to be here in the middle of the night. She seems so sophisticated and otherworldly. Well, she and James, both. I'm more convinced than ever they're performers. Wouldn't it be amazing if they were famous? I've never met anyone famous.

Isabelle and the Americans tease James about his trousers and Isabelle offers her scarf for him to tie around his waist so he'd be decent walking up the road.

The Americans lead the way again, though I'm not sure they know where they're going. I follow them because, behind me, James and Isabelle are in a serious conversation. I catch only snippets, but wish I could hear it all, as I'm right about them being performers. Their voices mingle harmoniously as they discuss a play they're writing and want to perform. That much I understand. How exciting. I'm glad now that I came along.

The Americans stop at the corner.

"Hey, James, where to now?"

James's stunning voice travels through my body as he responds.

"Turn right. I'm coming."

We catch up to the Americans and James leads us down a side street with elegant houses I didn't expect to see.

James is fiddling with the scarf and trying to get his keys from his pocket. I'm surprised he didn't lose them as his pockets are hanging from the belt holding his trousers up. I can't imagine how he tore them that way.

Behind me, Isabelle's voice is soft but clear.

"Did you just stick my scarf up your bum, James? That's disgusting. You know I have to wear it later when I go home because I'll be cold without it."

James's belly laugh is contagious and we join in as he struggles to get his key to work in the door lock. I didn't realise how high he was until now. I watch his hands shake as he misses the lock several times before opening the door and switching on the light even though the first light of dawn is making its way through the windows.

The apartment is clean and tidy. James leads us to the kitchen and I grab a seat against the wall. My legs have had enough of walking. I'll deal with getting home later.

The Americans sit down too, but Isabelle remains standing near the door. I can feel her staring at me and without thinking, I offer her one of my beers. Thankfully, she refuses, but I notice the Americans eyeing the can in my hand. I don't want to share my beers with them, so pretend I didn't notice their expectant expressions, using the excuse of the early morning sun shining in my eyes.

James seems unaware of the small drama playing out in his kitchen. Instead, he gets rid of his torn trousers and t-shirt. His tiny blue undies leave nothing to the imagination, a fact not gone unnoticed by the Americans.

Spurred on by their attention, James goes into full-on acting mode. His beautiful voice reverberates through the room, and I suspect, the entire apartment, as he gives us a thrilling, dramatic rendition of Hamlet's speech, using a coffee mug for the skull. Just when I thought I couldn't be more impressed, he bursts into singing a wonderful song I'd never heard.

The Americans give him a standing ovation and ask about the song.

James jumps up on the countertop and sits, swinging his shapely legs.

"Well, darlings, that was an oldie from my days with Dancing with Wolves, a band I joined years ago, before I ever went to drama school. Singing has always been my passion."

The taller American turns around in his chair to see James better.

"That's awesome. What happened to the band?"

For a moment, James looks down and I fancy I see sadness in his expression. But when he looks up at us, his smile is back on his handsome face.

"You know how it goes. Promises, promises... We must have been quite good because we nearly got a contract with Warner, but alas, it wasn't to be."

James puts a dramatic hand over his forehead.

"Life had other plans for me, darlings. Instead, I went to drama school, then the Royal Academy of Music and that led me to meeting my gorgeous soul-sister here who cast me in the most fabulous show recently, saving my life and that's not too dramatic to say. And now I get to work with her on yet another brilliant play. Life works in mysterious and wonderful ways."

He has a twinkle in his eyes as he speaks and I get the impression he's flirting with the Americans.

I don't like it. I want his wonderful energy to be focused on me as it was when we walked up the road to the bus stop. It felt like I was the centre of his universe then, and starved as I was for such attention, it felt amazing to me. His warmth and focus on me was like the sun shining just for me. Now, he's taken it away and given it to these two men who aren't worthy of it.

Heat runs through my body. Fury builds inside me and I feel the Glome stirring in reaction to it.

I want the others to leave. James is mine, my friend. He chose me out of all the people at the bus stop. I don't want Isabelle to stay, either.

The Glome isn't peeping at anyone, but his presence is filling the kitchen. Though the sun is bright outside, and moments ago, shone happily through the window, the kitchen is now dark and cold.

I'm happy when I see the Americans shiver and get up, their smiles wiped from their stupid faces. Isabelle retrieves her scarf where James had discarded it over a chair along with his clothes.

Their voices are forced as they say goodbye to me and I notice none of them can look me in the eye. I don't care. I stay seated and drink my beer.

The Americans' voices disappear down the corridor as James leads them back to the front door.

I can just about hear their words.

"No, really, we must go. Our flight's at noon and it may take some time to get back to Heathrow. Lovely to meet you guys. Must stay in touch..."

James's voice carries clear to me, probably because it's an actor's trained voice.

"Why don't you stay, Isabelle, my lovely? You don't have to go yet, do you?"

Her voice carries clearly as well.

"I have to teach this afternoon, James, darling. You'll be alright. You have your friend here now. I'll see you for our usual rehearsal tomorrow afternoon."

James's voice is outside now.

"But I really want you to stay with me. Come back inside. You can leave in another hour or so, can't you? It'll give you plenty of time to get home to teach. Or you could just cancel the student? I don't want you to leave me."

Isabelle's laughter is like a bell, clear and bright, but I can tell she's lying. She's scared. That's why she's leaving.

"Oh, James, darling, we've been out all night. Aren't you tired? I'll just show the American guys where to get the bus and tube back to Heathrow and I'll be on my way. We'll see each other tomorrow. Don't party too hard today, okay? Our rehearsal will be full-on because Martin seems keen on helping us produce the play in the West End. We can't lose such an opportunity, don't you think?"

James's voice sounds defeated, like that of a little boy being told he can't have the toy he likes.

"Okay, I'll just walk you to the end of the road, then."

"You can't come outside like that, darling. You'll get arrested."

I can hear James's laugh is strained and I feel sorry for him. But I don't care that his friends are leaving.

"I'll just use this umbrella, my lovely. No one will see my face."

Isabelle's lovely, sparkly giggle fades as they walk away from the flat.

The silence in the kitchen is bliss. I drink my beer and enjoy the sun through the window. The Glome's darkness has retreated. For now.

CHAPTER 28

I MUST HAVE FALLEN asleep because I wake myself with a sudden, loud snore.

For moments, I'm disorientated.

Where am I?

Nothing is familiar. Not the chair I'm sitting in, the sun blazing through the partially open blinds or the sounds of traffic and people talking in the street outside, the smell of the incense-laden air, or the energy of the place that feels light and creative. One thing is obvious at once and I'm grateful for it. I'm no longer in prison.

I relax and breathe out.

The guy on the bed in front of me stirs. He's wearing only small, blue undies, visible because his sheet is bunched up around his thigh.

Ah, yes. I remember now. James... The guy I met last night at the bus stop. This is his place somewhere in South London.

Everything from the night before rushes back into my mind. I see the two Americans walking up the road towards the bus stop, their bitchy remarks to me, them ignoring me and running up the steps to the top of the bus, then rushing down it when the bus stopped, not caring that I might be left behind. Them playing with James, the woman and a shopping trolley. I remember borrowing money from her. What was her name?

I rub my hands over my eyes that feel gritty from too little sleep, too many drugs, too much booze and the need for a shower, while I wrack my brain for her name. How annoying. It's just at the edge of my mind.

The name slips into my head, or perhaps the Glome shares it, I don't know which, but ah, yes... Isabelle. That's her name. Such a pretty name.

In my mind's eye, I see her glancing at me as she hands over the money to James. Then I take off for the shop and later join them again to walk here, to his flat.

It all seems like a dream now and yet, it feels like I've known James forever.

I know the Glome scared away the Americans and Isabelle, but I don't feel guilty about it. Well, at least not about them leaving.

James is my friend now. We need to spend time together on our own, get to know each other. It can't be done with the others around, can it?

The Americans practically asked the Glome to scare them because of their shitty remarks about my weight and stuff. Serves them right.

But I feel a small twinge of guilt about Isabelle. She did nothing wrong. Still, she'll forgive James because she loves him. That was clear from the moment I met them, and it goes both ways. I can see James feels the same about her. How lucky they both are to have such great friends in each other.

Maybe I'll have that with James too, but I suspect not. I sense something else about our relationship, but can't quite solidify it. Perhaps it'll be revealed later, as we get to know each other better.

I shift in the chair and James's eyes fly open.

His voice sounds groggy and parched but surprisingly sober.

"Oh, hi. I didn't realise you were still here. Did you sleep in the chair the whole time?"

He sits up against the pillows behind him, yawns and stretches his arms above his head.

His beauty is blinding and I find I can't look away from him. It's not just his physical beauty, either. He seems to shine from the inside. I wonder if it's because he's a performer, perhaps part of their training?

I rub my forehead and run my hands through my hair which feels like it could do with a good wash. Prison isn't renowned for good hair care products or time enough in the showers to get rid of dirt and grease properly. I spent as little time as possible in the showers. The episode with Ned wasn't something I wanted to repeat. It will live with me for the rest of my life.

James's voice penetrates my thoughts.

"Are you hungry? I'm starved. But I don't think there's much in the way of food here. Let me change and we can go to the corner shop."

I get up and James tells me the way to the bathroom, having guessed what I needed.

By the time I return to his bedroom, James had dressed and made his bed. The room looks pristine.

I'm hungry, but the jitters dictate my need for more beers and ciggies. I hope James will get them for me and watch as he grabs his keys, the rucksack that seems glued to him, his bank card, and steers me down the corridor to the front door.

His hand feels warm and comforting on my back and I regret having to step through the door without it still being there.

James closes the door and I follow him down the short path to the gate.

He sounds sober for someone who'd consumed that many drugs last night.

"Right, let's go. My stomach is touching my spine I'm so hungry."

He must've seen my surprise for not locking the door.

But his smile and words reassure me.

"No need. We're only going to the corner shop and back. I'm not even taking my phone. No one will enter in our absence."

Guess I'm still in prison mode, where doors must be locked at all times. The minor act of not locking his door is an immense gift James doesn't even know he's giving me. The freedom I feel lifts my spirit at once.

I can see the shop from his street, but we're not there yet when my phone pings.

I glance at the screen. It's a message from my dentist.

Damn, I'd forgotten about my appointment today and I can't miss it. It took loads of people to set up the appointment and my brother will kill me because he's already paid a deposit for it.

My breathing increases and the tightness in my stomach tells me I'm panicking. I catch up to James and grab his arm.

"Hey man, I have to go home. My dentist just sent a reminder. I have an appointment I can't miss. How do I get home from here and can I borrow money for tube and bus fares? I don't have any on me."

James doesn't seem fazed by my anxiety or my request. Instead, he gazes at me, his face frowning in thought.

"You've just reminded me, Lee. I've been having a pesky tooth problem for months now and I'm not registered with a dentist. Do you reckon your dentist will see me too? Where and when is your appointment?"

I glance at the message on my phone to confirm my appointment time. Though my stomach gets even tighter when I check the message again, I try to be calm and shrug.

"I don't see why not? Do you want to call them? The dentist is near my home in North London. I have to be there at two and it's twelve now. Do you think I'll get there in time?"

James scratches his chin. His stubble is darker than last night.

"Nah, let's just go. Maybe they'll see me when I turn up. It's worth a try. But I'm starved. Let's buy something to eat, first, then I'll order a taxi. It'll be the quickest way to get there."

I feel my insides rising inside me and almost heave with relief as I follow James into the shop. Choosing a packet of beers and some biscuits, I notice my hands shake as I take them from the shelves. At the till, I ask for the ciggies I want and watch James pay for our stuff with his card. He buys sandwiches, crisps and a Diet Coke.

Outside the shop, he borrows my phone and calls a taxi that arrives quickly. I scramble into the backseat and James follows.

He's tearing open a sandwich and taking a bite, speaking with his mouth full of food.

"Tell the guy where we're going, Lee."

Now I'm in the taxi and on my way, I relax a bit, blow out a breath and give the address to the driver before turning my attention to my biscuits and beer.

James offers me a tiny white tablet and a packet of sandwiches. I decline the food but take the tablet and swallow it down with a gulp of beer. It might calm me.

It's cooler in the taxi than outside. I like it but James has his window open so the warmer wind moves into the car along with smells and sounds foreign to me. It always amazes me that wherever I go in London, I find myself in an unfamiliar atmosphere. I don't always feel comfortable with it, but today, with James, I do. I feel as though all is right with the world, even though I still need a shower and sleep. But I'm on my way home. My key burns in my jeans pocket.

I've stopped panicking but check the time as we stop often and speed far less than I'd like, through unknown-to-me London streets. When we reach a familiar park in North London, I sit back and realise I've been fooling myself until now. I had been freaking out. Even the sandwich James offered couldn't entice me to relax, and I'm not sure the tablet has worked yet.

The taxi drops us off outside my dentist and I'm happy we're fifteen minutes early. It means James can talk to the receptionist and try to get an appointment for himself while I wait for mine.

Only one other person sits in the plush reception area. I'm assuming there's more than one dentist, which should mean I'd be seen quickly. How long my appointment will last, though, I didn't know and wondered if James would wait for me. Our time together doesn't seem long enough yet. I sense we still have lots to talk about, much to learn about each other, and briefly wonder why it feels so important. But I'm too tired to think about it further. It's wonderful that James is here with me.

I notice James flirting with the receptionist. His stunning, musical voice rings through the space as he laughs and chats with her. Her quick words and giggles tell me she's clearly taken with him, too. Moments later, when he slips into the chair beside me, he says despite his best efforts, they could only see him tomorrow and suggests spending the night at my place. Did I mind?

Did I mind?

It's exactly what I wanted and now, my dream came true without me having to do anything or risking rejection by asking him to stay.

I feel my face stretch wide as my smile pops out of me.

"Sure. It'll be fun."

When the dental nurse comes to collect me, James once again moves to resume his chat with the receptionist.

I envy his easy way with people and his ability to get such fantastic responses from them. Even the dental nurse blushes when James winks at her. Don't they realise he's gay?

But soon, thoughts of James flirting with girls disappear as I concentrate on the dentist's fingers in my mouth and all the gadgets he's using in there. The sound of the drill is horrendous and I grip the sides of the dentist's chair, my eyes shut tight, ankles crossed and pressed against each other to absorb my anxiety.

I don't know how long I was with the dentist, but it feels like ages. When I'm finally released from the torture, James is still smiling and chatting with the receptionist.

He looks up as I return to the reception area. His eyes change from flirty, sparkling blue to the dark blue of concern.

"You alright, Lee? Looking a bit pale there, mate."

He takes my arm, waves goodbye to the receptionist, and steers me outside. James and I notice the pub on the corner at the same time and we head towards it.

It's one of those typical pubs with flowers in hanging baskets around the front and wooden tables outside. We make our way inside where the welcome smell of stale beer combines with a sticky carpet to greet us.

Only two older blokes sit on stools at the bar. It's probably too early in the day for people with busy lives to be here, and I'm grateful. I feel woozy from the dental visit.

A table near the window catches my eye. I take a seat there and watch James at the bar, getting our drinks. I know he knows by now I'm a beer man, but I wonder what he drinks since he's only been taking drugs so far. His rucksack must be a small pharmacy, judging by the never-ending supply from there. But I'm grateful because whatever the drugs are, they still my jitters, even if only for a while.

James plonks a pint in front of me and takes a seat opposite, a glass of red in his hand.

"So, Lee. Do you live nearby? I have no idea where I am, though I've been to North London before when Isabelle and I rehearse at her place or at Abney Park Cemetary. It's a hoot. I should take you there sometime. You'll love it."

How James knows I like the peculiar silence found only in cemeteries, I'll never know. But he's right, of course, and I'm excited he's thinking of our relationship in the future. Despite our backgrounds being similar, he's so far out of my usual friend zone, I didn't dare hope he'd be interested.

I take a gulp of beer and sit back, trying to play it cool.

"Yeah, I've heard of it. Sure, it'll be great going there with you sometime."

James and I share more of our stories, drink more, take tablets and eat crisps. James is so different from Ned or anyone else I know. I'm happier than I've been in a long time. Even the Glome is purring inside me, like a huge, black, dangerous leopard.

The guy appearing at James's side startles me.

"Hey, gorgeous. I thought it was you I saw through the window. Fancy running into you here."

James's eyes light up as he recognises his friend. He gets up to face the man who has tattoos running up his neck and peeping out on his forearms where his shirt sleeves are rolled up.

"Hey, Scott. Good to see you, darling. Want to join us?"

Scott kisses James on the mouth and touches the side of his face.

"Lovely to see you, but I popped in when I noticed you through the window, babe. Just on my way to a job."

I'm fascinated by the ring through Scott's nose, but when his eyes run over me, I feel his disapproval.

He kisses James again and walks away backwards, holding his hand up to his ear, fingers imitating a phone.

"Call me, okay?"

James waves and sits down again.

"Scott's an old friend. I'd forgotten he lives and works in North London. Shame he can't join us."

James looks temporarily disappointed about Scott's departure. But resumes the story he'd been telling me. His good humour returns and soon, we're laughing at the hilarity with which he'd escaped a disastrous show in Spain before Isabelle cast him in her show.

I don't know where the time went, but when I look up, I'm surprised to see lights have been switched on inside and outside the pub. My stomach growls and I know I have to get home straight away. There's no food at the flat, so we'd have to make another detour. I can hardly face it because I'm so tired and my legs still ache from all the walking last night to the bus stop and then to James's place.

But as we leave the pub, James must have sensed my gloom because he becomes even more animated, chatting and gesturing.

When we reach a row of bushes, I duck behind them to relieve myself and when I step back onto the pavement, there's no sign of James. Perhaps he had to take a leak too and went somewhere nearby.

I wait for a few minutes, but when he still doesn't show up, I start walking. The hunger pain in my stomach transports me back to times when panic rose in my chest at the thought I wouldn't be able to sate it. Even now, I feel the terror and lengthen my strides.

Suddenly, James jumps out from behind a tree and scares me half to death. He thinks it's funny and cackles like a demented hag. But I stand frozen for a few moments and then push past him. I can't be doing with such childishness, no matter how much I like him. I need food, my meds, and sleep.

How he still has so much energy is beyond me. Must be the drugs because he continues to eat them like they're sweets, dipping his hand into the rucksack every few minutes. Perhaps he's so used to them, he needs to take a lot before he feels their effect. He offers me one every time he takes one, but I'm done. I just want to get home and I'm getting more and more frustrated with him and having to go to the shop for food first. His staying over at mine might not be a great idea after all. But he's paying for stuff, so I'll have to accept his silly games.

Unable to get the desired reaction out of me, James pretend-scare me several more times as we walk up the road.

The Glome is aware of my change of mood and rises to the surface. I'm even more pissed off because now I have to deal with the Glome and everything else and all I want to do is go home, eat something, take my meds and sit down in peace. I hope Barry had been paying all my bills so there will be electricity and I can watch the telly. But seeing James's antics, I doubt he'd sit still long enough to watch the telly with me.

I don't know how I got through it, but I'm almost overwhelmed with relief when I finally get my key into the lock on my front door and push it open, allowing James to go ahead of me. He's got bags with our food and, as the flat is so small, finds the kitchenette at once.

My hands shake a little when I flip the switch and light floods the flat. I let out a breath and make a note in my mind to thank Barry tomorrow. The place smells a little musty and carries an unlived-in atmosphere, but it's still my home with the things I recognise.

I follow James to the kitchenette and pull out the only two plates I have, tablespoons and forks for us with which to serve and eat our dinner. In the drawers, I find my meds and pull out the plastic bags, place them on the coffee table in front of the sofa.

But I'm too hungry to care about being hospitable and dive into my meal, swallowing every mouthful down with more beer. Beside me on the sofa, James is enjoying his meal too, but without the beers. We wolf down our food, I take my meds and when I've finished, I'm so tired, I can't even get up to put my plate in the sink. But James clears up and cleans everything in the kitchen until it's cleaner than when we arrived. He even washes the floor.

Where does he get his energy from? We hardly slept last night and, to be honest, prison for the last three years had not been the most restful place. Exhaustion hits me like a hammer blow and I feel myself slipping into the abyss of sleep.

I'm not sure what wakes me. But I'm instantly aware it's very late and I haven't finished sleeping yet, the grip of sleep still tight around my body. I force my eyes open and see James sitting on the sofa next to me, his eyes glued to the telly as he's stuffing tablets into his mouth, one after the other. My meds are strewn all over the coffee table, but there's a lot more than I remember, and I'm sure he must have placed his tablets there as well. For moments, I feel the heat of annoyance surging inside me. How am I supposed to separate my meds from his? How thoughtless of him.

I struggle to get up, but I manage and stumble to the bathroom. I relieve myself and splash cold water on my face to wake up, but it has no effect on the fatigue that lives in my bones and makes me feel heavier than I am.

James should sleep, so I can get some rest. I go back into the open-plan living room/kitchenette and grab stuff out of the small wardrobe against the wall.

"Hey, James. I'll put my sleeping bag and duvet over here for you to sleep, okay?"

He looks up from the telly, his Scottish accent a little thicker when he speaks.

"That's grand, thanks."

He gets up and takes off his shoes, T-shirt and jeans. I'm impressed that he folds the clothes neatly and places them at the foot of the makeshift bed on the floor beside the wall.

Sleep threatens to overtake me. I stumble back to the sofa and collapse on it. As though I'm already dreaming, I'm aware of James finding a glass and filling it with water in the kitchenette, draining it and getting into his bed. But he's not there for very long. I hear him getting up and going to the bathroom, closing the door.

When I open my eyes again, it's morning, but I know it's too early to get up. The sun shines through the window to my right, gleaming off the TV's screen.

James isn't in his bed and I'm assuming he's had to use the bathroom. I need to go badly too, probably from all the beer last night. I shut my eyes again and wait for him to finish. But the minutes tick by and
everything's quiet in the flat. I can't hear him in the bathroom. Perhaps he's left, but I notice his clothes and shoes still in the neat pile where he'd left them last night.

I don't want to pee in the kitchen sink, so I get up and walk to the bathroom. The door is closed.

I knock. No response.

"James? Are you in there? You okay?"

Still no response, though I think I hear a groan. I push down the handle and find the door unlocked, open it and go inside.

James is sitting on the loo, his head on his arms resting on his thighs.

I can smell he's made a poo, but he's not moving. Is he asleep? I push his shoulder, but he doesn't move or speak.

"Hey, man, are you okay? I need the loo."

I notice he's been sick on the floor and there's sick in the basin. Nausea rises in my throat, but I swallow it down. I don't want to add to the mess.

Suddenly, I'm angry.

I'll have to clean all this up and I don't even like cleaning my own fluids.

The mystery that had so impressed me when I first met James has become old and I'm more irritated than I've ever felt.

I push him again and still, there's no response from him.

How rude.

I grab his arms and try to pull him from the loo. But he's far heavier than he appears, and I struggle to get him off the seat. I'm guessing it's because of his muscled physique. Muscles weigh more than fat, I've been told. He also feels hot and I hope he's not ill with a bug he's passed on to me.

I do my best, but I can't hold James. He slips from me and falls to his knees beside the loo with a loud crunch. I wince as I imagine how sore his knees will be when he wakes up.

When I go to use the loo, I see he's filled it to the brim. Again, nausea rises in me, but averting my face and pinching my nose, I flush it and notice he's somehow broken the seat.

My anger is waking me.

Looking at James's inert figure on the floor, I realise he hasn't cleaned himself. I rinse the basin to get rid of the sick there and grab some toilet paper to wet and wipe James's bum, pull up his blue undies before I clean the floor in front of the loo.

Still, James hasn't woken, though he's groaned several times. He doesn't look comfy, kneeling on the tiles like that with his head bowed under his chest. But I don't know how to help him and I need to relieve myself. I can't wait for him to wake up and leave the bathroom so I can have privacy, so I go with him on the floor next to me.

When I've finished, I flush the loo and can't help being annoyed that he's broken the seat that now sits at an angle. Another thing to deal with when he's gone.

I push him again.

"James? Are you okay?"

A faint groan is his only answer.

I don't have the strength to lift him again. I'm suddenly heavy with renewed exhaustion, so I leave him there and go back to the sofa, pulling my t-shirt over my eyes to block out the sunlight as I sink back into sleep.

This time, when I wake up, my lips feel glued together. They're so dry and my tongue feels swollen. I get up and go to the sink to get water. The glass James had used last night still sits on the counter, so I use the only other one I have. I gulp down the water, feeling it run down my chin and wet my t-shirt, but I don't care. I fill the glass again and drink it down again. The water feels cool as it goes down and stills my hunger a little.

Only now do I notice James isn't in his bed, but his clothes are still in the pile he'd left last night. Sounds from outside tell me it's later in the morning and people are on their way to work as they walk past my window on the pavement below.

James can't still be in the bathroom. Could he have fallen asleep in there?

But when I get to the bathroom, the door is closed. I can't remember if I'd closed it last night, or if he's been out and gone back in again.

I knock.

No response.

"James? Are you in there? Are you okay?"

I press my ear against the door but hear nothing. I open it.

James is in the same position on the floor where I'd left him and appears to be asleep. Must be the drugs that knocked him out in such an awkward position.

I go to him.

"James?"

He's completely still.

I try again, louder this time.

"James, wake up."

But he doesn't respond.

I touch his shoulder and, as I do so, feel the icy cold of his body beneath my fingers.

I hear my voice as if from far away.

"No, no, no. This can't be happening. I can't go back to prison. No. God help me!"

I struggle to breathe.

Maybe I'm not awake. Maybe this is just a dream.

But I know.

James is dead.

CHAPTER 29

I DON'T KNOW WHAT to do and I can't think. This is bad, worse than anything that's ever happened to me.

My heart's racing and a tight knot sits in my stomach. The nausea returns and I have no option but to vomit in the loo next to James's cold body. I do it quickly, flush the loo and get out, stumbling over my feet and shutting the door behind me.

What to do? What to do?

I can't think, can't get my brain to work.

Pacing my small flat, I'm pounding my chest with both hands. My face hurts from being screwed up, and tears drip down my chin. I'm cursing in my head, at James and at the Glome. He feels like a menacing, dark storm threatening but not doing anything. How can he forsake me now when I need him most?

Breathing is difficult through the tears and snot, and my body feels too heavy to keep moving. I plonk down on the sofa, my head in my hands, my body shaking and heaving as I continue to cry.

What am I going to do? I'm going back to prison for sure and this time, it's forever. I can almost taste the heavy stink of the place in the back of my throat. I mean, no one's going to believe me, are they? James died in my flat. I should have tried harder to get him back to his bed when I found him earlier. But would that have helped?

What to do? What to do?

I can't sit still either. Scanning the room as though something will miraculously appear to help me, I see the pack of unopened beers sitting on the counter in the kitchenette.

I get up and grab the pack, open it, and swig down a beer. It helps. I feel somewhat calmer as the warmth of the liquid reaches my stomach. Squashing the empty can, I throw it into the trash. At least I've stopped crying.

What will the police do when they come?

I try to see my home through their eyes.

As I haven't been here for three years, the place is relatively clean. Only the makeshift bed I'd created for James seems out of place. Then my eyes land on the coffee table in front of the sofa and the mess James had left mixing the tablets. How will I know mine from his? They're all jumbled together.

I get up, grab and carry the rest of the beers to the sofa and sit down again, but I don't touch the tablets or the coffee table. Maybe it's evidence that James was the only one who created this chaos and took all those tablets. Thank God I took my meds last night before he messed it all up.

The beers help to clear my mind and calm me, and though I feel fuzzy from lack of sleep, I can think straight. The digits on the telly say it's nine o'clock.

I wonder when the police will get here. But even as the thought forms in my head, I realise I'd have to call them. No one else is going to do it. No one else is here. I'm alone in my flat with a dead guy in my bathroom. The episode with Ned in the cell flashes through my mind. Panic races through my body at once.

I can't go to prison again and I can't be in solitary again. I just can't.

Tears come without my permission and drip down my face, mingling with snot running from my nose. I use my T-shirt to wipe it all away. No way can I go back into the bathroom to get toilet paper for the job.

I'm angry at James for messing up my life again, at myself for letting him stay over, at the Glome for being stubbornly silent when I need him and for not knowing how to deal with this situation that will not go away on its own.

Barry would know what to do, but can I trust him? It wasn't like I'd known James for ages and then I went ahead and trusted him, and look at the result. I can't contact Grandfather. He'd be completely clueless.

With a heavy sigh, I retrieve my phone from my back pocket. Looks like I'll have to call the police myself, but what's their number? It's either 999 or 911, but which is American and which is British? I blame American movies for my confusion. It probably doesn't make a difference. Both numbers are for emergencies. I dial 911 and wait. Nothing. Not even a ringing tone. I try 999 and someone answers at once.

"999. What's your emergency?"

I know I must speak, but my voice doesn't want to work.

The woman's voice repeats the question.

"This is 999. What's your emergency?"

I feel the Glome rise inside me and take over my voice.

"My friend died in my bathroom last night. I think it was a drug overdose. I found him there this morning."

She asks my address, and the Glome gives it.

When the call is finished, I'm sweating and shaking but grateful for the Glome's help. He's hovering, silent again, but seems calmer than I feel.

I'm hungry but we ate all the food last night, so I drink the beer instead.

It seems like hours go by before I hear heavy footsteps coming up the stairs and then the banging on my front door.

Going to open the door feels like I'm walking into a situation I'll never escape again. But I have no choice.

The police and ambulance arrived together and while two policemen ask me questions, other people are going in and out of my bathroom, checking the tablets on the coffee table and doing forensic stuff I'd seen on the telly.

I answer the questions as best as I can, but I know the look in the policemen's eyes. They don't believe me. I don't blame them because they can probably hear the fear and anger in my voice. The Glome is quiet again, and I have to deal with this by myself. I don't understand it. Why isn't he supporting me?

It's not a surprise when the policemen cuff me and walk me downstairs to the waiting cop van. But my stomach sinks when I see the people at the corner shop out on the pavement, staring. Even if by some miracle I'm released, how will I live here again now? Everyone will think of me as a criminal. I feel my face flush as I remember all the times I'd nicked food and biscuits from the shop. They may already regard me as a thief because the last few times I went there, they were on to me. But I ignored them and marched out of the shop with my loot before anyone could stop me. I'm much bigger than any of the girls working there. What could they do to stop me? Call the police, I suppose.

Well, the police are here now. I'm cuffed and on my way to jail. Again. I've only been out for a day and two nights. How much bad luck can happen to one person? I had nothing to do with any of the things I've been imprisoned for, including James's death.

At the station, I tell the cops I'm hungry and I need my meds, but they just ignore me and I'm left alone in an interrogation room.

I feel sick. Why do I never get a break? Is it the Glome's doing? But to be honest, I'm positive he wasn't responsible for James's death. It feels more like the Glome's gone AWOL, except I'm aware of his dark, lurking presence inside me.

I'm even less hopeful I'll get out of here, when a while later, two stern police officers enter the room, together with a guy called John. He's my lawyer, the man informs me as he shakes my hand. They take their seats opposite me and question me for what feels like several hours. John's interruptions make it feel even longer, but I get why he's doing it. He's trying to help me and I'm grateful someone is. God only knows what's happened to the Glome, my constant companion.

My body feels like I'm floating. I'm so tired by the time they finish with me and lock me up in a cell for the night. The familiar prison smells and sounds seep through the bars and echoes around the small room as I lie on the narrow, hard bed, my arms behind my head for comfort. My stomach responds aloud to the aroma of food that drifts towards me. At least I'll get something warm to eat.

TWO WEEKS LATER, I squint and blink as I step into the blinding sunlight outside the prison. I've been released. It means either John did a good job, or they must believe I didn't kill James and had nothing to do with his death.

I walk away from the building as fast as I can, up the street that leads to a main road I can see from here. I'm sure I'll get my bearings once I know where I am. Having no money on me, I'll have to walk home.

Several hours later, I struggle to get the key in my front door, pick up a small yellow sticky note that's been stuck in the doorframe, and stagger into my flat. I'm too exhausted to care that all the lights had been left on while I was in prison.

In the kitchenette, I grab a glass, hold it under the tap until full, then gulp down the cool, slightly chlorine-tasting water. I drain two glasses of water before I feel less shaky and dehydrated.

The makeshift bed I'd created for James is still in the same place, but his clothes and shoes are gone. The police must have taken it.

I want to use the bathroom, but I don't want to go inside. Instead, I walk there and peer through the door the police and paramedics had left open. The bathroom looks as it's always done, except the seat on the loo is lopsided and I can't stop seeing James's crumpled body beside it in my mind's eye.

Weirdly, I feel proud of myself that I'd cleaned him and pulled his undies back up. It's the least I could have done for him, so he could be seen with dignity by strangers who met him only in death.

There's nothing for it. I go to undo the strings on my trackie bottoms and realise I've stuck the yellow sticky note I'd found in my door to the back of my hand. I pull it off my hand to read the message.

Hi, Lee. You may remember me. I'm Isabelle. You met me the same night you met James. I've learned James was with you when he died. I hope you're okay. It can't be easy. Call me if you need to talk. Isabelle.

I see her phone number at the end of her message.

My pulse beats against my temples.

How did she find me? Did the police give her my address? Surely, that's illegal. I'll have to call John. He'll know what to do.

I shove the sticky note into my pocket. Anger rises up into my chest and I almost forget why I'm in the bathroom.

I relieve myself quickly and wash my hands in the basin. There's no towel, so I dry them on my t-shirt and trackie bottoms. I leave as fast as I can, close the door and breathe out when I enter the living room.

I take the sticky note out of my pocket and read the message again. A tight feeling sits in my chest. I'm not sure if it's anger or fear. Where's the Glome when I need him?

Somehow, I'd assumed the whole sad story would end with the removal of James's body from my bathroom and having done my time in jail. This has gone on longer than expected.

I'll have to call Isabelle back, but what can I say? I realise they loved each other. Would she believe I had nothing to do with James's death?

As soon as the thought pops into my head, the tightness in my chest constricts and I know fear has made a home inside me.

I'm hungry, but how can I go to the corner shop now? They saw me being arrested. I'm broke and will need to take food again without paying for it. They'll certainly be monitoring me more closely now and I just can't face getting into more trouble with the police.

I text Barry, who texts back at once, promising to pop around with food, beer and ciggies. His text sounds suitably remorseful for not looking after me properly. He apologises for not getting me the money he'd promised to arrange through a government scheme for people like me.

By the time Barry arrives carrying several shopping bags, I've washed in the sink because I can't face the bathroom, cleaned my clothes and put on fresh ones from my wardrobe. But I don't feel any better inside myself. The Glome is still silent as though he's sulking and I feel the most depressed I'd ever been, even during all the time I'd spent in prison.

Barry doesn't stay. He unpacks the groceries and finds places for everything in the fridge and cupboards. I take the ciggies, lighter and a beer with me to my place on the sofa. Barry promises to get me money soon and also a place on a plumbing training scheme. I'm only half-listening and half-remembering the test I had to do that showed my abilities and led to the choice of training as a plumber.

I notice Barry's eyes flitting towards the bathroom as he talks and moves quickly towards the front door, apparently eager to leave as soon as he can. It suits me because I'm too tired to deal with anything or anyone. But the sticky note burns in my pocket and I know I must call Isabelle.

I gulp down several beers and when I feel calmer, I key Isabelle's number into my phone, click call. May as well get it over with sooner.

After three rings, she answers. I recognise her beautiful voice at once.

"Hello?"

I clear my throat.

"It's Lee. You left a note at my flat. How did you know where I live?"

I know I sound rude, but I don't care. I just want it all to end.

Isabelle seems to ignore the obtuse note in my voice as she responds.

"Oh, hi, Lee. I'm so glad you called. Being with James when he died must have been so hard."

I'm silent as I contemplate her words. Is this why I'm feeling so low?

"Why are you harassing me? I didn't kill your friend. How did you find me?"

"Lee, I'm not harassing you. I'm trying to help. My friend Victoria, who also knew James, is psychic. That's how I found you."

I don't know if I can believe her.

"Do you want me to kill myself? Is that what you want?"

Her voice slaps me.

"No!"

Kindness returns to her tone.

"You have it all wrong. Please don't hurt yourself. I don't blame you for James's death, darling. The only reason I contacted you was to check that you're alright."

Before I can say something, she continues.

"Shall I pop around? Would you like me to bring food and wine?"

More food would be helpful because whatever Barry brought won't be enough.

I speak quickly before Isabelle changes her mind.

"Yes, that would be grand, thanks. Can you bring a burger 'n chips too?"

Her voice is clear, like a bell, and perhaps I'm imagining it, but she sounds relieved.

"Sure. Anything else?"

I tell her the brand of ciggies, beer and chocolate biscuits I want and end the call.

It feels like ants are crawling under my skin and I know it's my jitters, getting out of hand. I need my meds. Thankfully, the police forensic guys had separated my meds from James's tablets and returned mine. Switching on the telly, I pop two pills and swallow them down with some beer. I run through the channels on the telly, but nothing seems interesting and I don't really want to get into anything because Isabelle said she'd be about an hour.

The taste of an imaginary burger and chips makes me salivate and occupies my mind instead. But no matter how many times I look at the clock, the minutes seem to crawl by.

Isabelle's voice replays in my head. She's right. I need to talk about James. There's been no one who'd understood the impact James had on me. But Isabelle will understand and perhaps her psychic friend will, too.

I must have fallen asleep because the sound of knocking wakes me up and I know at once it's Isabelle at the front door. Pushing myself from the sofa, I shuffle to open it and let her in.

She looks just as lovely as she did when I first met her, but an immense cloud of sorrow surrounds her and her eyes are the saddest I've ever seen. Another woman behind her must be the psychic friend, Victoria. I feel instantly on my guard. Who knows what she can see in me? Would she see the Glome?

I stand aside to let them in and they walk the few steps to the open-plan living room/kitchenette, where Isabelle deposits the bags of food on the counter.

The smell of burgers and chips wafts through the flat and I can hardly contain my excitement at having it.

Isabelle must see how hungry I am because she encourages me to eat, saying they'd already had their dinner. But I remember my manners and offer them tea.

Only Victoria accepts tea and I make it quickly while checking what else they'd brought. Meanwhile, Isabelle drinks an apple drink directly from the small bottle she brought along for herself.

The bags contain my burger and chips, chocolate biscuits, more ciggies and beers and a bottle of red. I don't have wine glasses and pour the wine directly into my beer glass, take the burger and chips and return to my spot on the sofa.

While I eat, Victoria explains how she saw James in a weird position in a bathroom. When she 'tuned into him' – whatever that means, apparently, he led her here to my flat. Isabelle takes over the story to tell me how they'd come to see me one evening and left the sticky note when I wasn't home.

Their story sounds legit and I relax. Everything that's happened to me after meeting James has been surreal. Now, for the first time, since I got to live on my own in this flat, two women sit here chatting to me as though they don't fear me or the Glome, or think less of me because I'm not of their world.

Victoria says something that takes me aback until I remember she's psychic.

"Do you think James's death was because of drugs, by accident, or by design, Lee?"

No one's asked me that question and though I'm not sure what she means by 'design,' I guess her point.

"I'm not too sure. We took the same drugs and though I drank more beer than the drugs, it's scary that he died and I didn't."

An image of James sitting in Victoria's place flashes through my mind. I see his fevered eyes glued to the telly while his fingers glide over the coffee table, searching for the next tablet. He reminded me of how I sometimes eat chocolate biscuits one after another until they're all gone. But I don't share the vision with the women.

When Isabelle stands, saying it's time to leave, I can't believe how time flew. I don't want them to leave because I enjoyed their company, even though I didn't think I would. But I don't want to be alone in the flat tonight.

Pushing myself from the sofa, I stand.

"Can you drop me off at a pub I like in Edgeware?"

I notice the quick look between the women, but it means nothing to me. Perhaps they're coming to an agreement about who will drop me off.

While I run a comb through my hair and grab my jacket, Victoria moves towards the bathroom door. I've kept it closed, so I don't have to look into it every time I come and go from the front door. But the heaviness of James's presence hasn't gone just because the door is closed. It appears to grow stronger by the day, instead.

Victoria stares at the door as she speaks.

"Would you mind showing us the bathroom, Lee? I'd like to see how much of my vision was correct."

Everything in me goes still. For some reason, I don't want to show them the bathroom. The police and paramedics trampled all over the place, but somehow, the bathroom feels like a secret between James and me. I try to play for time, combing my hair again, putting some moisturiser on my face, talking about the pub I like. But I can see neither Isabelle nor Victoria is buying my act. Their eyes show they're waiting for me to give them what they want.

Time is running out. If we don't go soon, I'll miss the pub because closing time is at eleven o'clock.

Both women are standing near the bathroom door, expectant faces watching me.

I sigh and open the door. I don't want to go inside, stand aside so they can enter instead. Isabelle follows Victoria into the room and I stay standing in the doorway. They march to the spot James died.

Victoria turns back to me.

"It was here, wasn't it? He died here?"

There's no point in hiding anything from them any longer. But my voice sounds strained and nervous.

"Yeah. That's where he died."

Victoria stares at me for moments before she continues.

"He was in a weird position, wasn't he? Like he was kneeling with his head almost under his chest and his arms by his side."

I nod.

Victoria's eyes scare me because she seems to look right through me. I glance at Isabelle, but she's deep in thought and the sadness around her has increased even more. I don't want to see her eyes and turn away, bend down and pretend to tie my shoelaces, instead.

The women's silence makes me uncomfortable. I find my key and stand near the front door, waiting for them. Moments later, they leave the bathroom and we leave my flat, still in silence, the kind that honours the dead.

Outside, Victoria leads me to her car and Isabelle follows us in hers.

I reckon it was a fair exchange, them seeing the bathroom in return for taking me to the pub. But as we turn onto the main road, Victoria glances at me.

"I know you wanted to go to a pub in Edgeware, Lee. But it's too far away and too late now. We'll get there after the pub's closed. So, I'll drop you at the pub on the corner, okay?"

I'm disappointed, but Victoria's right. We won't get there in time for me to have even a quick pint. Victoria is kind enough to give me a ride, though I could have walked to the pub. My lips involuntarily thin in annoyance, but I remember my manners and thank her when she stops. I get out of the car. Isabelle waves to me as she drives by behind Victoria.

I lift my hand but don't wave back, turn and enter the pub. It's the same pub James and I visited before he died. It's exactly why I didn't want to come here. But at least there's still time to get in a few pints.

The place is packed. It's a Friday, so expected.

I wonder if it means I'll get away without paying for my pints. Barry still hasn't sorted the money and I have very little left which I must use for food.

Someone taps me on my shoulder.

"Hey, aren't you James's friend?"

I turn around and recognise the face, but can't place the guy. He's got tattoos crawling up his neck and peeping out from under rolled-up shirt sleeves. Light glitters off his nose ring.

The guy thrusts a hand at me.

"Scott. I remember you were sitting at the window table with James the other day when I passed here. Lee, right?"

I remember him now, how he kissed James and called him 'babe.' Perhaps he was one of James's lovers.

Oh, man, how do I tell him James has died?

CHAPTER 30

I'M REELING FROM THE scenes I just watched of my life.
But it seems to have happened to someone else, not to me.
I suppose I was someone else in my physical life, and I find it
impossible now to reconcile myself with that me.

My thoughts must have spilled out because the energy of
the others surrounding me expand expectantly. Their curiosity
fills the surrounding space. But I understand at once their
brightening isn't about the events of my life we just witnessed.
Instead, they're more interested in my reactions, what I've
learned from what happened, and who I'm becoming. I sense
all these things simultaneously.

As I look down at myself, I see my body resembles the energy
of the others now. A light shines through the diaphanous form
that used to be my physical body, as though it's coming from
within me and expands to just outside the barely visible outline
of my form. It reminds me of James's earlier question about
Angels. I wonder if this is what they look like.

What do I know of Angels? Can't say I've ever really giv-
en them much thought. Though we were supposed to be

Catholic and Grandmother sometimes went to church, tried to drag us along, we weren't religious.

The being I saw before I died, who took the Glome, seemed like an Angel. But I have no frame of reference.

I turn my energy towards James and try to adjust to the way I feel in my new state.

I continue our conversation as though the snippets from my physical existence didn't just interrupt us, my way of buying moments to understand what lies beyond it, I suppose.

"Angels never featured in my life."

A thought I'm not sure I like enters my mind.

"You don't mean the Glome is an Angel, do you?"

The silence that follows fills me with a dread that I might be right about the Glome. What kind of Angel behaves like that? The silence lasts for moments before I feel the others' energy around me increase in intensity. They know something, but either can't or won't tell me.

James flashes brighter as he turns towards me.

"Angels aren't only associated with man-made religions, Lee. Angels are beings with their own functions and paths to expansion. Remember, we're all evolving. What happens to one of us, happens to all, and that includes Angels to an extent, as they too, are part of the Consciousness."

Why is he talking about Angels as if the Glome isn't one of them? Surely, they can all read my thoughts and know it's what I'm thinking. Why is no one confirming my suspicions about the Glome? I always thought the Glome was evil. Can Angels be evil?

The soul who identified as the man with the dark hair flares beside me, and I know his thoughts are directed at me. A familiarity about him strikes me now that hadn't earlier. Then, recognition.

If I could, I would gasp. It's Ned. Only now do I recognise him, or perhaps my ability to see things more clearly has increased? I know the being that was Ned in the physical feels my shock, but he seems unperturbed by my reaction.

"Nothing is evil, Lee. No such thing exists in all of creation. It's the ego's interpretation, condemnation and judgement of actions that lead to the conclusion something or someone is evil. Only experiences exist through energy, vibration and frequency. Those are the only things in existence."

I know with every fibre of my being, his words are the truth. But I can't help being confused. How do bad things translate into energy, vibration and frequency? I have an idea it's all necessary for the growth of all. My mind is spinning trying to work out how Angels fit into this.

James's presence next to me grows brighter again as he directs his thoughts to me.

"Angels are the only beings in creation that aren't born, Lee. They're created, fully formed, and fully aware. You must have heard of such things as Guardian Angels?"

I'm preoccupied thinking about Ned being here, and also still wondering about the impossibility that the Glome might be an Angel. But now, James throws an even scarier idea into the mix. Could the Glome have been my Guardian Angel? Is this talk of Angels to prepare me to meet the Glome here?

Such a thought in my physical life would have me sweating and shaking with fear and trepidation. But all I feel here is curiosity and the otherness of perhaps meeting the Glome properly at last. Finding out who or what he truly is would answer a lot of questions.

The Love that surrounds and envelops me in its golden light fills me with conviction I'm safe here. Nothing can harm me, not even the Glome.

I'm unsurprised when James continues, as though he knows exactly what I'm thinking.

"Lee, we'll get to the Glome and answer all your questions. But for now, it's important you understand the role you played in something far more significant and yes, the Glome was part of it. Let me explain."

I focus all my attention on James. But I feel the others' energies leaning in and detect their barely concealed enthusiasm for this part of the unfolding story.

James hovers in front of me.

"In rare instances, fragments of the Consciousness, who want to accept a more penetrating role, may choose to transform permanently as Angels. It's a rare and complicated procedure."

I want to focus on James's words, but the more he imparts, the more the Glome remains at the back of my mind.

James's incredible voice draws me in and again, I'm staggered by the intense light emanating from him. He seems to have grown in stature, too.

"You may have guessed by now, Lee, that I have chosen to become an Angel. I understand fully my choice is irreversible, but I know this is how I can be of the highest, truest service to humanity and Consciousness. My transformation began several lifetimes ago and yes, you were part of them all. We were both preparing for my complete transition into the Angelic realm. But we needed extra help. It's where the Glome, as you call it, came in and also where your help was needed."

I'd be speechless in my physical form. None of what James just revealed ever entered my mind. That I could have helped him to become an Angel? An Angel…? How is such a thing possible?

I'm reeling even more from this than from witnessing the craziness that was my physical life. This information is truly surreal. Did he say the Glome was needed too?

Before I can ask, James finds the question in my mind. He responds as he moves away, so the light that appears to expand from him and around him doesn't cut through mine.

"Becoming an Angel when one has been human is a tricky thing, Lee. Being human is the most challenging for any soul to negotiate. It's the densest incarnation where souls who choose it can make the biggest impact in the Consciousness's expansion. To go from that lowest of vibrations to the highest frequency, which is that of the Angelic realm, is not only difficult but also perilous. It's a process, and I needed someone I could trust entirely. So, I split myself into three fragments - you, me and Isabelle. Each of us had a role to play in helping me bring my dream to fruition. It would be my last dream as a soul capable of incarnating as a human. I know you may be wondering about Isabelle and her role?"

James must sense my astonishment because he continues.

"Isabelle must stay human for now. She's not aware her actions in the physical, are helping me here. But not all souls can incarnate into the density of the physical dimension, nor would they want to. Those of us who do, are brave, special and capable of doing so much to affect creation for the good of all."

I'm silent. It's a lot to take in. I didn't know being human was special, but all those programmes I'd watched on the telly about aliens, come to mind. I'd always wondered why aliens, who seemed so much more advanced than humans, would hang around the Earth. It would make sense if they're jealous that they somehow can't incarnate as humans. But to be honest, I never felt special in my physical form as a human at all. James's words make me feel better about it at once and I'm grateful when he resumes.

"Lee, you may find it difficult to remember now, but you'd agreed to play the biggest role in my transformation. If not for you, neither I nor all of humanity would benefit from my decision."

I wait for him to say more, but he's silent and I realise he's waiting for my response.

"I'm genuinely surprised by everything you've told me, James. But I don't know what I did to help you. I'm only glad I did. For the last days and months of my life, I felt so bad about your death and often wondered if there was something I could have done to prevent it. My life felt so much less important than yours.

James's energy reaches out to me and I'm aware of an instant calm washing through me at his touch.

"No life is more important than another, Lee. It's only the human ego that deems it so. But we're all necessary for the growth of all as we're one Consciousness. It's important that you understand that, Lee. Even as fragments of my soul, Isabelle and you were equal to all. However, your decision to help me and your permission to allow another fragment to meld with you in your physical form makes you unique. Our experiment – for that's what it was – could have failed."

Curiosity overcomes me, and I have to ask.

"What would have happened if we'd failed?"

James's energy brightens before he answers and again, I get the sense he's upgraded from the energy I knew as James.

"Nothing as bad as you might imagine, Lee. We would have come together again as one and continued our cycle of reincarnation together as a whole until we overcame all challenges the physical experience could provide. Then, we would live here as an integrated ascended master to help others."

I can't help being astonished.

"You make it sound like we succeeded?"

James joins with the others' smiles as their rainbow sounds float through me.

"Indeed, Lee. My metamorphosis into the Angelic realm has already begun. It started the moment you died. It's why you had to watch your physical life until the end, so you could witness the part you played in my transformation."

I'd nod if I could. Instead, I feel my energy intensify as I've noticed the others do when directing their thoughts to each other.

Mine is directed at James.

"But what about the Glome? Where does he fit in?"

James is brighter than any of us and he seems much taller, or perhaps I'm imagining things.

"Not the Glome, Lee, but an aspect of Azrael, known to humans as the Angel of Death. In our reality, he's the Keeper of the Truth, the Supreme Grandmaster of Transformation. Without his help, neither of us could have succeeded, Lee.

Some Guardian Angels seem fierce and dark, but they're often our greatest protectors and their actions are often unfathomable to us in our physical forms."

Yes, the Glome protected me, my Guardian Angel, Azrael. But I can't forget how he attacked me.

CHAPTER 31

D UST MOATS FLOAT IN the sunbeams shining through John's office window.

Why would anyone want to be a lawyer?

His office is a mess, with papers strewn everywhere and files stacked in piles. It reminds me somewhat of Grandfather's newspaper mountains.

I'm trying to concentrate on John's words, but in my mind's eye, I see the pack of beers sitting on my kitchen counter, waiting for me.

What's an Inquest, anyway? I can't be bothered to ask, but it seems important when John insists I must be there and I'll have to go on the stand, swear on a bible and be a witness to James's death.

To be honest, I'm sick of the entire business around James's death. I just wish it would go away.

Beside me, Barry is making frantic notes on his phone as John drones on. I know Barry will grill me later.

By the time we leave John's office, it's already past lunch and my stomach growls loudly in the elevator, much to Barry's embarrassment, when the two girls behind us giggle at the noise. I don't care. I need food and Barry takes me to the greasy spoon across the road for a full English fry-up.

Barry's face is serious as he speaks through a mouthful of food.

"You must get a family member to accompany you, Lee. I can't be with you on that day."

I nod, but can't imagine who I could ask. Grandfather won't come, so there's no point in even asking. Conor and Mary haven't forgiven me for not going to Liverpool to attend Grandmother's funeral. I couldn't bring myself to go, and anyway, Conor's business was too important. There's no way he'll come to London just for the Inquest. I'll have to persuade Mary, but it won't be easy. We've spoken little since Mother's funeral and I can feel her disapproval through the ether whenever I call her. I can't really blame her. It seems I'm always in trouble, as I'm always calling her from prison.

When I tell Barry I'll talk to Mary, he backs off a little. But he pulls out his phone and goes over the phrases and words I'm supposed to use during my turn on the witness stand. It's legal jargon and I make my own notes so I can remember the words on the day.

Barry drops me off at home and I call Mary's number as I climb the stairs to my flat. It rings for ages. Just as I'm about to end the call, she answers.

Her voice sounds irritated and cold.

"Hello, Lee. Where are you?"

I can't help the sniff as tears well up in my eyes. It's so good to hear her voice, even if she's mad at me.

"Hello, Mary. I'm just walking into my flat. I need to ask you a favour. Are you still working in London?"

I try to concentrate on Mary's words as I open my door, but I've never been one for multitasking. Sitting down in front of my door and leaning my back against it, I continue my conversation with Mary. After I remind her how I'd saved her life that day with the truck in the road and how it would be good if she could do me this one favour, she finally agrees, albeit reluctantly, to come to the Inquest Court with me. I know it means she has to take time off work and I appreciate it even more for that reason.

The silence after our conversation is comforting and I stay in the same position for moments before pushing myself up and opening my front door.

An immediate heaviness meets me as I walk into the flat. Since James's death, a weird feeling has inhabited the place, which is why I try to spend as much time out as possible. But the morning's meeting with John and Barry has wiped me out and I must have my nap. I feel drowsy from a full stomach, and my tablets add to my inability to keep my eyes open for much longer.

The beers on the kitchen counter catch my eye and I take them to my spot on the sofa, switch on the telly and scroll through the channels until I find something about walking in the Lake District. The presenter's voice is just the kind that will help me drift off to sleep.

M ARY INSISTED I WEAR a tie and jacket with my trousers, not a suit exactly, but it will do. She came to collect me earlier than I expected.

It's a good job I was already up and had washed and peed in the kitchen sink, scrubbing it afterwards. I can't face going into the bathroom at all now. The weird, dark energy in there makes me nauseous.

But it's probably a good thing that we're first at the Court. The Clerk of the Court shows us where to wait and I can feel Mary's disapproving eyes roaming over me. But I don't look at her. I'm reading the words and phrases on my phone that John said I must use and Barry passed on from the notes he'd made.

When more people arrive, I look up but don't recognise any of them. Two women with pale faces take seats opposite me and a man with a bald head joins them moments later. I guess they must be James's family, but only the young woman resembles him. A sister, perhaps?

Then I hear Isabelle's bright voice as she and Victoria enter the waiting room. Behind them, follow three more men, and I know they're gay at once. More friends of James's, no doubt. At least they seem friendly. The other lot doesn't smile or talk to anyone.

Isabelle and I exchange glances and she smiles at me. I return her smile and make a gesture to suggest going for a pint later. I'm hoping she'll take me home because Mary won't be able to stay for the entire event. She said she'd leave once I'm done.

Before long, we're called to enter the Courtroom and now I understand the two women are James's mother and sister. The bald guy was his flatmate. They're sitting near the witness stand and I'm already sweating, knowing their eyes will hate me.

Mary and I take our seats with the others in a row of chairs further away. I'm trying to stay calm, but I see my knuckles are white on the chair's arms when I look down.

Some medical people go first. I watch as they swear an oath on a bible, holding up the other hand and saying something about 'telling the truth, the whole truth and nothing but the truth.'

What does that even mean? I just hope I remember the words I'm meant to use for the questions the Coroner will ask.

I don't listen to the two men called to the witness stand separately. But my ear catches something about James having been prescribed sixteen tablets per day. That's a lot, much more than my prescription. No wonder he died.

Then, it's my turn. My knees feel like water when I walk to the podium. I look at Mary, but she's texting on her phone.

A mantra in my head sings loud.

I don't want to go back to jail. No, no, no. I don't want to go back to jail.

The Coroner asks questions that sound like he wants me to admit I'd killed James. But I didn't. I'm shaking.

Suddenly, the Glome takes over my voice and I almost crumple from the relief. The Glome remembers all the phrases John suggested with ease. I hear him saying words I'd never use, like 'I recall' instead of plain 'I remember.' The Glome stresses the point that I'd not found James earlier when he was still alive, as it was a good job I didn't need the loo sooner.

I'm not sure that's true, but the Glome knows what he's doing, so I let him say whatever he wants.

My grin of triumph as I get off the podium stretches over my face. I walk back to my seat next to Mary and touch her arm to celebrate my victory. I'm not going back to jail. It's over. It's finally over. But she's not smiling. Her eyes are dark and accusatory.

Before the next person gets called to the podium, Mary gathers her things, whispers she has to leave, and hurries through the door.

I'm alone again.

But I feel the Glome vibrating inside me. He's celebrating with me. Later, we'll get to drink to our success when we join Isabelle and James's friends at the pub across the road.

When it's all over, I leave as soon as possible and stand in the street outside the Court, smoking to calm myself. Even with the Glome's help, this was a nerve-wracking experience I do not wish to repeat. I'm finally released from everything to do with James, and I'm ready to celebrate my freedom.

But when Isabelle and her friends emerge, their faces are white and pinched. I reckon they need a drink more than me.

Isabelle walks towards me.

"I'm sorry Lee. We're absolutely bushed and won't join you for a drink. We're going home now. Good to see you."

She waves as they walk away around the corner, leaving me standing with my cigarette halfway to my mouth.

What the actual...! How am I meant to get home now?

My jubilation evaporates somewhat as I contemplate my journey back by bus. But there's nothing for it. Cursing under my breath, I saunter to the nearest bus stop. I may as well head home too, even though it's still early afternoon. There's no fun drinking in a strange pub by myself and I'll have to take at least three buses to get me home. Who knows how long that will take?

The bus drops me off near the pub on the corner where James and I went that time. I stand for moments trying to choose between going home or going to the pub. I'm hungry and the pub will have hot food.

It's a good thing Barry had arranged a proper income for me. The only drawback is he's teaching me how to budget, so the money lasts all month. But today doesn't count. I deserve a treat.

The joy I felt earlier about not going back to jail resurfaces, and I take long strides towards the pub.

Drawn to the table where James and I had sat that day, I choose it when I placed my order and collected my beer. The table is at the centre of a window that overlooks the park on the opposite side of the road. Perhaps that's why I like it. The scene is peaceful, and the pub is relatively quiet, as most people are still at work.

It's never bothered me eating by myself and it doesn't today, either. I listen to the song on the speakers while I eat and realise it's the same song that was played that time I was here with James. It's catchy. I like it. It will probably always remind me of James. Interesting that I feel so relieved thinking about him now. Gone is the anguish, anger and guilt I'd felt for his death.

I sit back in the chair, having finished my meal, thinking about what the future holds for me now. It feels like a blank page, waiting for me to write the story of my life. Barry had arranged a plumber's training course starting next week and though I didn't think I'd like the idea, I realise I'm looking forward to it. Doing something useful with my life should be fulfilling and perhaps even fun. But the daily discipline of work makes me think of prison.

A waiter collects my plate and empty beer glass. The place is filling up with people and I don't want to give up my table but I want another beer, so would have to go to the bar to get one. But just as I push my chair back to get up, someone taps my shoulder.

Looking up, I see Scott standing beside me.

"Hey, Lee. I thought it was you. You disappeared so quickly the other night. Are you okay? You looked a bit peaky that time."

I can feel my smile is weak and my good mood has disappeared.

"Yeah, I'm okay, thanks. Needed to get home that night, but everything's okay now."

I pray Scott knows James has died. Perhaps the friends I saw at the Courthouse told him. I don't want to be the one to break such news to him. My heart sinks in my chest because Scott seems too cheerful for someone who discovered a good friend has died.

Scott nods towards my empty glass.

"Want another? What's your tipple?"

I tell him my order, and he comes back with two pints. He hands me mine and sits down opposite me, where James sat that day. For moments, we drink in silence, though the level of noise around us has increased as more people entered the pub.

I lean towards Scott to hear him over the din as he speaks.

"Where's James today? It was so weird seeing him here the other day. I didn't realise he ever came to North London. Doesn't he live on the other side of the river?"

I could tell him now, but I still don't know how. So, I play for time.

"Well, he told me he rehearses in North London for a new play every week. So, he's here a lot from what I understood."

Scott nods and eyes me over the rim of his glass as he takes another mouthful of his beer before he speaks again.

"How did you guys meet?"

I can't blame him for such a question. It's obvious James and I were worlds apart in every way and the most unlikely friends.

I tell Scott about how I'd met James at a bus stop and he roars with laughter.

"That's our James. No offence, but he was always collecting strays, stray people, stray animals... Did you know once he even had a stray fox in his flat for a while until the thing bit him? He has the kindest heart of anyone I know. Where is he anyway, do you know? I've been calling him for the last few days and he's not responding, most unusual for him."

Shit, I'll have to tell Scott. But I don't think this is the right place. Instead, I ask if Scott wants to come to mine.

"Sure, why not? It's very noisy in here tonight. Must be some footie game on later, judging by the scarfs people are wearing."

We down our beers and walk out into the darkening evening. I need to get home, anyway. It's time for my tablets.

To delay telling Scott about James's death until we get to my place, I ask him the same question he'd asked me earlier.

"So, Scott, how did you meet James?"

As Scott tells me about the hilarious episode of how he'd created a theatre costume for James and how James had split the trousers on stage, I notice Scott is carrying a similar rucksack to the one James had. I also can't help spotting Scott dipping into the rucksack regularly and putting something into his mouth. He's not chewing it, whatever it is, so I doubt it's sweets. His actions remind me of James's and I wonder if it's drugs, but I don't ask.

Scott's energy is high and reminds me of James's, but it's not as chaotic and unexpected as I'd experienced with James that night. Scott seems more steady though his sense of humour reminds me of James's.

As I open the door to my flat, Scott asks to use the bathroom and I point at the closed bathroom door, hoping it's okay since I haven't been in there in weeks.

I go to the kitchenette, take a quick piss in the sink and scrub it before I open the drawer that contains my tablets. Holding a glass under the running water from the tap, I fill it before walking to my place on the sofa, carrying both tablets and water in my hands.

It's a while before I wonder what's keeping Scott. I can't hear him in the bathroom and he's been in there for some time.

An icy hand clamps over my heart.

Not again.

But just as I'm about to go into full-on panic mode, Scott reappears. His face is ashen and his eyes are dark, almost black, but I can't tell if it's from the drugs he's clearly been taking.

Scott throws his rucksack on the sofa beside him as he plonks down on the other end of it.

"There's some weird energy in your bathroom, man. Doesn't it freak you out?"

I can't delay any longer. I speak fast as I tell Scott what happened that night, that James is dead.

A long silence follows my confession. A distant ambulance siren is the only sound.

I wait for the condemnation I'll see when Scott faces me, but when he looks up, his eyes are enormous and tears are streaming down his cheeks, running into the tattoos on his neck. I've never seen someone cry like that before, as though the tears are separate from his emotions, yet there they are.

He gets a tissue from his rucksack and wipes his eyes, blows his nose, shakes his head.

"It's not what I expected to hear today. But now James's silence makes sense. I thought I'd pissed him off somehow."

I'm still waiting for Scott to scream at me for keeping this news from him until we got here. Instead, he stares at me with what I read as compassion in his eyes.

His voice is soft and sad when he speaks.

"I can't believe you lived with this all by yourself, Lee. It must have been so difficult."

His words remind me of Isabelle's and once again, I'm touched by how kind James's friends are. They say 'birds of a feather flock together,' don't they? James must have been a truly remarkable human being. Sadness that I never got to know him better, sits in my heart.

Scott rummages in his rucksack and pulls out several packets of pills, offering them to me.

"Want some? They may help."

He doesn't wait for me to respond. Instead, he opens a foil and takes out a tablet, which he places in his mouth. Looking around, I guess he's looking for something with which to swallow it and I hand him my half-full glass of water, which he takes. He swallows the tablet down and pushes the packets towards me on the sofa.

I take one and offer him one of mine. It's the least I can do. He even bought me a beer earlier, didn't he?

As we chat and laugh, I'm reminded of the night James spent here. But this is different. Scott is more settled and doesn't jump up and down every few seconds like James did. Scott doesn't pace as he speaks, either. He remains sitting on the sofa, facing me, and we talk like we've always known each other.

But something feels off. I'm woozy and my tongue doesn't want to work properly. I know what I want to say, but the sounds that come out aren't always words. Scott doesn't seem to notice. He's talking non-stop and taking the tablets every few seconds. In that regard, he's like James. I'm not sure what he's talking about, but I like that there's another voice in my flat.

The dizziness increases and now I'm feeling nauseous, too.

"Sorry man, I've just got to go to the loo. Won't be long."

I push myself from the sofa but feel I'm unsteady as I make my way to the bathroom.

Can't piss in the sink with Scott here. Plus, I feel I'm going to be sick. I'm somewhat trepidatious as I enter the bathroom and stand still for moments. But nothing happens and I feel nothing sinister lurking in the corners.

I relieve myself and feel disgusted that I'd missed the toilet bowl a little. Will have to wash the floor again.

I still feel like I'm going to be sick, so I hang around, but nothing happens. Perhaps if I stick my finger down my throat, I'll be sick and then I'll feel better. I try it, but other than gagging sounds, nothing comes out.

I can hear Scott has switched on the telly and he's watching some game show judging by the sporadic laughter and applause reaching me through the closed bathroom door.

Nausea rises again. I feel like I'm in an alternate reality, and the feeling inside me is the only real thing. I still can't vomit, no matter how far I stick my finger down my throat. The more I do it, the more the nausea turns into pain that gets worse by the second.

When I can't stand the pain anymore, it shoots up from my stomach into my chest and I feel the world turning black around me. But I don't faint, I'm not allowed the luxury of that relief. Instead, I feel every single nanosecond of the Glome pulling out of my body. My eyes won't shut no matter how hard I try and, unlike the last time the Glome left my body, this time, I'm forced to watch and feel everything he has to dish out, as though he's punishing me.

The room gets darker as he fills the space around me. He's enormous. But when I think that's all of him, more painful streams of his blackness draw out from my solar plexus.

I know I'm making sounds and it feels like I'm screaming, but I can't hear myself. Instead, my hearing is filled with a massive rushing sound like a thundering waterfall as the Glome continues to withdraw himself from my body. Strings of his black filaments pull out of my arms, legs, hands, even my feet. My body is on fire and freezing simultaneously. As the Glome's form solidifies in front of me, his eyes are red, fierce and penetrating as though it's trying to annihilate me. Pure hatred pours from him and I can't help cowering in the corner, the same one, ironically, where James had died.

The Glome is massive, far bigger than I could ever have imagined. For a moment, I wonder how something that enormous could fit inside me, even when I was a baby. Did it grow with me, or was it always that big? But I feel too dizzy to give such questions much attention. Instead, I'm concentrating on staying upright against the wall.

I try to cover my ears as the thundering sound the Glome makes intensifies, then turns into a multi-layered scream. It sounds like thousands of people are yelling at the top of their voices, over and over.

I'm clutching my head.

Make it stop. Make it stop.

But it doesn't stop. Instead, the Glome rushes at me, roaring, his mouth wider than normal, teeth sharp and dripping with green liquid. He comes closer and closer and his familiar musky odour fills my nose.

Searing pain erupts at the side of my head as he bites off my ear. I can see it in his mouth as he throws his head back and the screams pour from him again, but this time, even louder than before.

Long talons pierce my skin and shred my arms as he lifts me, and throws me against the opposite wall. Spots of intense lights spear my eyes as my head connects with the tiles and I hear them crush beneath my weight. But he's not finished with me yet. Agonising pain shoots through my ankle as he grabs me there and throws me against another wall as though I'm a rag doll. I hear my shoulder break and feel debris fall on me from the broken tiles and mirror. Everything hurts, but I feel strangely disconnected from my body, as though I'm floating.

A loud, sharp bang accompanies the brightest light I've ever seen. It appears directly behind the Glome and for moments, I think I must be hallucinating because I could swear it's James. But it can't be. The being behind the Glome shines brighter than the sun. It's far bigger than the Glome, and massive wings tower above its head. Its energy and eyes are those of James, but I know I must be wrong. Unconditional love and compassion stream from the being towards me, even though I have to shield my eyes against its blinding light.

Before I have time to focus on it properly, it grabs the Glome in a tight embrace. They struggle for seconds before disappearing as though neither ever existed.

The sudden silence is deafening, but in the far distance, I can still hear the telly. How amazing all this happened and Scott didn't come to investigate the noise.

I know I'm close to death. My body is broken and I feel freezing. But a lightness I've never experienced runs through me. So, this is what I feel like being just myself without the Glome's presence inside me. Overwhelming gratitude fills me for the chance to know it even just this once before I leave my body.

My heart stutters and I know it's time. When my breath leaves me for the last time, and I feel myself lift away from my physical body, I'm contented that I did what I came here to do, even though I don't know how I know it or what it was. I feel whole for the first time.

CHAPTER 32

I KNOW I'M SAFE now, but watching my death was a harrowing experience. It would have been horrible to see anyone die like that but to know it was my death...

The question pops out of me.

"Why did he attack me like that?"

My question isn't aimed at anyone specifically, but I'm not surprised when James's energy flares brightly next to me. He seems taller and am I imagining wings of light stretching above his head?

As soon as James's thought message reaches me, I know he's right.

"The Glome, as you called him, became infuriated that by taking all those drugs you allowed yourself to die, Lee, and therefore robbed him of the opportunity to continue enjoying the world through you."

I knew it. Somewhere inside me, I knew the truth, even while it was happening. It's why I wasn't angry or tried to fight back. I couldn't have fought back, anyway. Who could defend against such a powerful being as Azrael? It was also obvious to me Azrael knew it was my time to go.

I replay the scene in my head.

But James fought him. I know it was James.

I'm still contemplating how the Glome or Azrael - now I know his name - could be my protector, my Guardian Angel and an aspect of the Angel of Death simultaneously.

James's focused thoughts penetrate my musings.

"Yes, Lee. It was me you saw battling Azrael. It was my ultimate test to complete my transformation."

I replay the scene again, seeing how James grabbed Azrael, and both disappeared through a rip in the fabric of reality. My senses picked up more than I remember, because now, as I focus on the image in my mind's eye, I see massive black wings towering above Azrael as James dragged him into the other dimension.

The young girl's energy, who was Mother, blazes to my side.

"Not all Angels are gentle, Lee. Some are fierce and ruthless in human terms, but all serve the Consciousness perfectly, including Azrael."

No sooner do her thoughts penetrate me, leaving me wondering if it means I'll meet Azrael here than an almighty thunderclap makes me jump. But nothing in the Love that surrounds me changes, so I know I'm still safe.

Moments later, I notice another, immensely powerful energy having joined our circle. No one need tell me of Azrael's arrival. His presence confirms he must be an Angel because how else could he be here in the Love? Yet knowing what I know of him, it seems impossible.

My senses are still overwhelmed by the Love that permeates everything, but I recognise Azrael's energy at once. Nothing dark emanates from him, however. His form is blinding, and he's massive, far taller than the beings that brought me here. I understand now they're Angels too.

Now Azrael is here our environment transforms. Gone is the theatre and in its place we're in a vast, open space. It's white, bright and beautifully decorated. A myriad of galaxies swirls all around us as though we're at the centre of the universe. Perhaps the loud sound I heard earlier transported us here somehow. But no one seems disturbed by the change. They appear to have expected it and obviously, it's not their first encounter with an Angel like Azrael.

The energy that was the older man with the long white hair and beard blazes and before his thoughts reach me, I recognise him. It's Uncle, the one the Glome protected Conor, Mary and me from. The one the Glome killed. But the man was more than Uncle, wasn't he? He was my biological father, I understood it even as the Glome killed him, and I was but a baby.

Thoughts from the energy that used to be Uncle, penetrate me.

"We all agreed to help, Lee. But you took on the biggest task, and we knew how difficult it would be for you. It's why we all surrounded you with love in the physical, even though it may not have felt that way. My task was to make sure you were conceived and I'm so proud of you, Lee. James's transformation isn't into that of an ordinary Angel, but rather that of an Archangel, and that doesn't happen for aeons. No one was brave enough to carry the Angel of Death inside a physical body so a new Archangel could be created. Can you see why James says without you, none of this could have happened? Because of you, not only will James become an Archangel that will help humanity, but all of Consciousness has received the biggest, most important expansion for aeons."

I'd be speechless if I was still in my physical body. It's not what I expected. Becoming an Angel must be scary enough, but becoming an Archangel is something else. I can't help but have renewed respect for James's bravery. Now his selfless compassion and pure spirit make complete sense. I remember thinking he was shining from the inside out, even in his physical form, all of it to prepare for this monumental task ahead of him.

The energy who was the woman with the flaming hair flashes on my other side.

"Indeed, Lee. That's why we went along with your plans. It was a hard life, but it had to be that, otherwise none of this could have happened. You see that now, don't you?"

As I recognise her energy, a rainbow of smiles that contain hers, too, reaches me. Grandmother's love, warmth and joy wash over and through me, and I'm grateful she's here with us too. I feel no condemnation from her for not attending her funeral.

A sudden stillness shows a shift in vibration and I know, without knowing how, that Azrael is about to touch my mind with his thoughts. Instead, I feel his emotions hitting me as hard as anything I've ever experienced. I thought I'd be terrified, but I'm calm, continuing to feel safe and loved.

Fury, anger and hate are superseded by joy, fun, laughter, tears, sadness, all the emotions I'd experienced in my life, but magnified to a monstrous degree. I understand it's his way of thanking me for the experience and also saying farewell. We'll never meet each other again. In my physical form, I may have felt some sadness, but now I feel only love. I send it to him and in return, he sends an overwhelming sense of warmth washing through me.

Azrael seems to have grown in stature even more. He's enormous. Vast wings tower above his head. But what's even more astonishing is the entity beside him who is even bigger and who shines with such blinding, piercing light, its form is entirely obscured.

As the being grows even brighter, I understand it's James. His transformation appears complete. His thoughts reach me but the colours, sound, light, scent and emotions that hit me at the same moment, are beyond anything I could have imagined.

"You may choose now, Lee. You can remain here, reincarnate, or reunite with my energy as the fragment of my soul that you are."

It never occurred to me I'd have so many options. I thought I had no choice but to either reincarnate or reunite with James's energy. But the Love is like a balm to my soul, a drug to my being. It's an ecstasy I don't want to leave. I want to stay here forever.

Before I send my thought response to James, he seems to know my answer.

Enormous, powerful emotions emanate from James, flowing through me. It's the most definite confirmation that my decision is the right one for me.

I'm aware of how the circle of my soul tribe draws together as we witness James expand, his form burning blinding white.

Massive wings expand far above him before he turns slowly into the brightest blue. The healing colour perfectly signifies his purpose as an Archangel. A strong smell of something that reminds me of lavender, swirls around us as James and Azrael leave us through a portal clearly visible above us. For moments, it appears all dimensions have opened through this portal, and I catch a glimpse of Isabelle. She's more beautiful than I remember, laughing and happy in the embrace of a stunning man. Love pours between them and into them and if I could, I'd gasp at the incredible beauty of love in that physicality, which I never even suspected while I was there. Their love undulates in myriad colours, stretches out far beyond them both, beyond the Earth, beyond their solar system into the centre of the universe, permeating everything it touches. If it's true for them, it's also true for all who love. I know it with the knowingness when you just know something, and you don't know how you know it.

Love is indeed the universal language.

As the breach between dimensions closes again and only galaxies swim around one another, James gives me one last gift. His name... The Archangel Curael.

I bask in the Love that envelops me and holds me in its overwhelming embrace. I'm at utter peace.

The thing that was wrong with me was what was most right with me.

If you enjoyed *The Sense of Other*, you might also like the previous novels in the *Love Beyond Reason* series, *The Healing Touch* and *Forever and Ever Love*.

You will make this author enormously happy with your short review on Amazon, Goodreads, BookBub or wherever you've bought your copy stating why you liked the novel. I cannot stress how important reviews are. They enable novels like *The Sense of Other* to live in the world and be enjoyed by other readers who would also appreciate your feedback. Plus the algorithms love reviews! But seriously, reviews can make an author's career.

UK Review link

https://www.amazon.co.uk/review/create-review/B0CBKNQT5Y

US Review Link

https://www.amazon.com/review/create-review/B0CBKN-QT5Y

FROM ANGELINA

Building a relationship with my readers is the very best thing about writing. So, please feel free to subscribe to my Newsletter - https://angelinakalahari.com/contact/ Or if you prefer, at Bookfunnel https://dl.bookfunnel.com/s95ua3lobb

You can also email me at angelina@angelinakalahari.com.

You'll receive occasional email notifications about freebies, new stories and novels, YouTube videos, podcasts, short stories and much more.

The first thing you'll receive upon subscribing is an exclusive novella called *Diary of Naomi, a Desert Elephant* - it's the story of what happens to ellie Naomi.

> *Elephants in Namibia are the toughest in Africa. But orphaned elephants are the toughest still. And they need to be.*

*All elephants must travel great distances to find
food to live on and they're renowned for their mag-
nificent memories and deep emotions.*

We first come across ellie *Naomi in Under a Namibian Sky*.
In the novella, *Diary of Naomi, a Desert Elephant*, we discover what happens when she finds the people responsible for
making her an orphan.

On my website, https://angelinakalahari.com/ you'll find
lots about books - mine and other authors' books I enjoyed
reading. There are videos with readings from my books, short
stories and much more just waiting for you to enjoy.

***

Here are more places for you to connect with me:

https://www.amazon.com/Angelina-Kala-
hari/e/B014HLBJ2K

https://www.bookbub.com/authors/angelina-kalahari

https://www.instagram.com/angelinakalahari/

https://www.facebook.com/authorangelinakalahari/

http://www.youtube.com/c/AngelinaKalahari - I'd love you
to subscribe to my YouTube channel - it's where I post free au-
dio chapters of my books, talk about the themes and characters

in my books, interviews with other authors and chats about love.

ALSO BY ANGELINA KALAHARI

LOVE BEYOND REASON SERIES
(A Paranormal Women's Fiction Romance/Suspense series)
The Healing Touch
https://books2read.com/u/bOXPro

Forever and Ever Love
https://books2read.com/u/mVR9kM

STANDALONE SHORT STORIES/NOVELLAS
Draven & Other Stories
(Three Paranormal Romance stories in ebook and audiobook
formats)
https://books2read.com/u/ba6Xnx

The Servitor – Paranormal Romance
https://books2read.com/u/bWp0lW

DESERT LOVE SERIES
(A Contemporary Romance series set in Namibia – happy endings)
Under A Namibian Sky
https://books2read.com/u/b5kWOp

Love in Modena – follow-on novella from Under a Namibian Sky (readers' request)
https://books2read.com/u/m2MqXk

Heat in the Desert
https://books2read.com/u/bprNGl

MIDDLE-GRADE NOVEL
George and the Gargoyle Who Lived in the Garden
https://books2read.com/u/4A7Age

NONFICTION
(Your Voice, Your Superpower, Series)
Breathing for Confidence
https://books2read.com/u/bw7N8P

MY AMAZING EDITING TEAM

Thank you to the best editorial team in the world - Julia Bakhmet, Susie Rix, Irma Troost, Elizabeth Dockrell-Tyler, Hester Human, and Clare Kissane - thank you so much for helping to create a wonderful story we can all be proud of.

ABOUT THE AUTHOR

Angelina Kalahari has worked for over thirty-five years as an operatic soprano, stage director and voice teacher around the world.

She received recognition for her contribution to the music, culture and economy of the UK from Queen Elizabeth II at Buckingham Palace.

Angelina has always regarded herself as a storyteller, either through music or through acting and directing. She honed her storytelling skills from a young age, writing and telling stories to her siblings at bedtime. It became a habit through the years and a solace while travelling for singing. She has many finished novels, children's stories and plays. Her publishing journey as an indie author began with *The Healing Touch*, a Women's Fiction novel, based on true events.

Born in Namibia, and having lived all over the world, she currently lives in London, UK, with her husband, her fur cat daughter, a rapidly diminishing population of house spiders and a smallish herd of dust bunnies.

She writes contemporary romance to explore love, women's fiction to understand love and middle-grade novels to give love. What more is there than love? But she has also recently come to the conclusion that drinking vast amounts of tea holds the key to life.